So Beautiful

So Beautiful
Ramona Dearing

The Porcupine's Quill

National Library of Canada Cataloguing in Publication

Dearing, Ramona, 1965–
So beautiful: stories/Ramona Dearing.

Short stories.
ISBN 0-88984-235-3

I. Title.

PS8607.E3786 2004   C813'.6   C2004-900509-X

1   2   3   4   •   06   05   04

Published by the Porcupine's Quill,
68 Main Street, Erin, Ontario NOB ITO.
www.sentex.net/~pql

Readied for the press by John Metcalf; copy edited by Doris Cowan.

Represented in Canada by the Literary Press Group.
Trade orders are available from University of Toronto Press.

We acknowledge the support of the Ontario Arts Council,
and the Canada Council for the Arts for our publishing program.
The financial support of the Government of Canada
through the Book Publishing Industry Development Program
is also gratefully acknowledged. Thanks, also, to the Government of
Ontario through the Ontario Media Development Corporation's
Ontario Book Initiative.

Canada Council
for the Arts

Conseil des Arts
du Canada

ONTARIO ARTS COUNCIL
CONSEIL DES ARTS DE L'ONTARIO

Canadä

For Doug Glover

❧ Table of Contents ❧

❧ Getting a Message ❧ Through to the Girl

Seeing as the wind is blowing straight into the sleeve of his jacket, it's strange that the inside of Lyle's right wrist – the part that makes him shudder if he thinks about it too long – isn't cold. The blood in his fingers throbs where the hot coffee makes contact. Double-cupped, from Tim's. Milk, no sugar. And he shouldn't be having the coffee, really. Fouls the gut. Makes the mind zoom. If his wife, Joan, saw him with it, she'd tease him about how he's always griping at everyone to stay away from the stuff, that it's pure poison. But it's still early – seven-thirty – and he needs something. Yesterday he went home shivery. Then again there was that bit of drizzle, not like today. Today is going to be a fine day once it gets going, warm enough by noon to feel sleepy when the sun pushes against his back. He can see his breath, and coffee steam coming through the mouth hole.

In the ravine the leaves are mostly yellow, one sugar maple gone red. No traffic noises down inside the bowl. Up ahead a man maybe half Lyle's age lets a St. Bernard and a black Lab off their leads. Lyle's grandson, Jeffrey, used to love coming here because of the dogs. He would point and laugh, even if they were growling and snapping at each other. When he was really little, he tried to catch up to them on his plastic trike. 'Sparky. Sparky,' Jeffrey would call to the dogs with that Boston accent all four-year-olds seem to have, but the only thing that came to him at a trot was his granddad.

Lyle slows down for a swallow of coffee but ends up having to hook his left hand into his breast pocket to get his hanky and wipe off his chin. A young woman in a track suit comes out of a side path that looks to go up through some trees and out onto the street. She's only half-jogging but she's breathing hard and saying something. Saying it again, to him. Saying she's just found a body.

'Pardon?'

'Back there.' She jerks her head in the direction of the path. 'You have to come.' She turns and takes a few fidgety, half-running steps back the way she came. Lyle doesn't move. She notices he's not following and she swings around. 'It's just a life or death thing, mister. Don't rush or anything.'

'Did you say someone's dead?'

She bounces out some nods and speaks louder as if it's just occurred to her he might be deaf. 'I'm saying it's a dead body, okay?'

She squats down on the ground hugging her knees. Lyle thinks about telling her to put her head down between her legs. Last thing he needs right now is a fainter, even though he figures she's all worked up over nothing. She's the excitable type, you can see it in how much she moves and twitches. He tells her he's going to get to a phone.

She stands up heavily. 'You've got to come with me. You've got to tell me if I'm nuts.'

Lyle looks around. The man with the dogs is out of sight. 'It's the police we're needing here.'

She starts crying, fast tears she squeegees away with the edge of her hand. 'No, you can't. It's in a garbage bag and what if we call the cops and it's just a bunch of crap in there? We have to make sure first.'

Lyle gets himself calm again. Of course it's garbage in that bag. You can't get a body into a Glad bag. This lady – more like a girl, really – took a scare. That's all. Maybe saw the bag at a funny angle or heard a branch snap behind her and got herself on the wrong end of common sense. Probably it's just the way the contents have settled and now she realizes she's made a regular thing into something to fear.

And he can understand how it's happened because he's done almost the same thing this morning, let his thoughts gunk up. The girl is black, and at first he thought she was setting him up for a robbery, that if he followed her into the trees he'd find several black men waiting. A rotten thing to think, now that he sees her upset like this.

'Okay,' he says.

'I always take the shortcut,' she's saying. 'I live right up there, so in the mornings I just scoot down and go for my run.'

Lyle is following her. She walks on tiptoe as if she can sneak up the side of the slope. He's still got the coffee but doesn't want it in his hand. Not that he's expecting trouble. But still, tying up the good hand – not smart. Should have dumped it in the garbage can they passed before turning off onto this path. They're walking up on at least a fifty-five-degree angle. The dirt is packed shiny with tree roots and rocks sticking out. He could put the coffee down here, it's not like there isn't other trash around. But what would she think, frightened the way she is already, with a man behind her suddenly stopping and bending down? Maybe she'd think he was getting a knife out of his pocket. Or his thing. What would she call it? Not penis. Cock, probably.

'Almost there,' she whispers, stopping to face him. 'You okay?'

He nods, raising the coffee in front of him as if greeting the neighbours when it's still too early in the morning to talk. He's got to stay on top of his reflexes. Otherwise, a person's just a bunch of routines.

You do things without even knowing. The first time Jeffrey ever slept over, Joan said, 'Look.' She'd been washing and Lyle had been drying. Jeffrey was right behind them, with a towel over his shoulder and a bath mat in his hands. At first Lyle couldn't see what Joan thought was so cute. And then he realized the boy was imitating him – Lyle always draped a spare tea towel over his shoulder in the kitchen. He gave Jeffrey a teaspoon to dry. Jeffrey scowled as he tried to press the bowl of the spoon into the bath mat. Joan got him a tea towel and they let him dry all the spoons and then paid their helper with ice-cream and cantaloupe.

The girl has stopped just up ahead and is looking at something on the ground. A hand behind her back gestures for him to come over.

It's a lawn bag, orange, with something big in it. But there's no way a body could be stuffed in there. Lyle can see where someone must have dumped the bag from higher up – they can't be far from the lip of the ravine. The bag's brought up on a tree, he can see that.

'Can you see his toes there?' she whispers. 'I was starting to wonder if I'd made this up and if you'd say I'm just winging out. But see his toes there, the outline?'

Lyle doesn't see an impression of toes or fingers or a bulge of head. The girl has quite the mind.

He steps toward the bag and stops about ten feet away. The girl stays behind him. He wants to tell her she'd show a lot more smarts to be afraid of him. Not that he's going to do anything. But how can she know that, alone with him where no one can see them?

'What are you doing?'

He's put the coffee in her hand and he's looking around for a stick. 'I'm going to open it,' he says, making sure the words come out sounding precise and flat, speaking at regular volume to counteract her whispers.

'Oh, Jesus.'

'Nothing in there. Nothing bad, anyway. You'll see.' He's got a short stub of branch and he tears the bag a little, except there's another lawn bag underneath. That bothers him a bit, so he touches the stick to one of the lumps, just enough to get a sense of what it feels like. That gets his heart going, all right. The girl is still behind him, still moaning, 'Oh, Jesus.'

He grabs the top of the bag, bends his knees like the doc keeps telling him to and lifts a little to get a sense of the weight. He gives the top a tug with his right thumb and forefinger wrapped around the yellow plastic tie.

Whatever's in there is heavy. When he steps back, he can see the outline of the foot she's been talking about. 'I think we'd better go,' he says to her.

She's almost at the bottom of the ravine by the time he's finished the words and she's yelling, 'Jesus. Help. Police.'

They stand next to the bench where Sergeant Tim Boland, Toronto Police Service, has told them to wait. The girl still has the coffee cup in her hand but doesn't seem to realize it.

'I hope it's not a lady,' Lyle says. The girl stares at him in a way that keeps him talking. 'I mean, if it's a male, you've got to figure he was probably running the wrong way somehow. To wind up like that.'

'He's black,' she says, arms folded. 'Ten to one, he's black.'

She says the words like she's slapping a face. The attitude's going to eat her up one day. Although it could be the shock. A life, a human breathing life, and it's been taken. And even though he thought he already understood this, there's an unpleasant buzzing in his head, the same kind he used to get when he was still going for syrup on his pancakes. Lyle waits for the girl to sit, his own legs aching. He's got to get into the sauerkraut again, the stuff is fantastic for circulation.

'Not that anyone should be killed,' he says. 'I'm not for that. Capital punishment and such.'

The girl paces behind the bench, head down. Finally Lyle sits and unzips his jacket a little.

She comes around to the front of the bench, scraping the soles of her sneakers on the side furthest away from him even though they don't have any mud on them.

'What would make this easier to take,' he says, 'since you're so young, would be if this was pretty much the worst thing that ever happened to you. I mean it would be bad enough but it wouldn't top you, you know?'

'You're some kind of freakiness, mister.'

He has no idea whether it's an insult, but he offers a Certs. Her shaky hand has a hard time retrieving it from his.

'This it for you?' she says.

'The worst?'

She bobs one of her springy nods.

'God, no.' He can see she was expecting him to say that but now she doesn't have the foggiest how to respond. She sits down.

Joan figured retirement would be it, that it would kill him. Said she herself was going to wait a year for him to adjust before she retires. Said she wasn't going to hold his hand while he cried two ways at once – about all the time he had on his hands and all the time he didn't have left. Which was a completely crackpot way to think Lyle would act. Sometimes he wonders how after all these years Joan could actually believe something like that. When has she ever seen him laid low? Keep moving and you're okay. He's got his walks, and enough junky furniture in the garage to keep him going until he croaks. You look at some old highboy and it's terrible and then you peel off the skunky paint and all of a sudden the thing's knocking you back with its dignity.

When Joan's cut free next year, they've been talking about taking Jeffrey to the Grand Canyon. He'll have turned nine by then, just old enough not to cry for his mommy every time they stop for gas.

Except there's a snag with those plans right now, a big one in that his daughter-in-law has disappeared and taken Jeffrey with her.

Lyle almost tells all this to the girl – he believes he owes her something for thinking those bad things about her earlier. But she'd probably think he's pathetic, an old guy looking for attention, siphoning her strength.

It's too hot, sitting there in the sun, by the time Sgt. Boland clomps down the hill to talk to Lyle and the girl. Her name is Letitia Holland. The officer keeps saying *L-i-t-e* and she keeps jumping in and saying, *No, l-E-t-i.* There aren't many questions, but the sergeant throws most of them at Lyle. See anything? Hear anything? Know anything that might help? The officer wants them to go to the station this afternoon to make formal statements.

Letitia calls him back as he's leaving. 'So what happened?'

Sgt. Boland looks surprised. 'Well, a homicide. For sure a homicide.'

'I mean, is it a guy?'

The officer says he's unable to disclose information pertaining to the investigation at this time, ma'am.

'Is he black? Is there going to be justice?'

Sgt. Boland shrugs and starts walking away.

She calls after him. 'I'm going to the funeral. Aren't you?'

Sgt. Boland stops, turns around. 'I can tell you folks we're not having a very good day.' He starts walking again, leaving a short shadow and a long silence.

They haven't gotten very far talking about the disappearance, Lyle and Joan and their son, Kevin. Lyle has asked Kevin the same question, over and over: What did you do to your own wife?

'Nothing,' Kevin said the first few times. But the last time, he said 'Fuck you,' and threw Lyle's reading glasses into the fireplace in the living room, where the flames from a chemical log were good and high, halfway up to the mantel holding

Joan's crystal bells and bowls and kitty-cats. 'Go get your eyes checked, Dad.'

Joan made Lyle sleep in the den for a couple of weeks after that. She stood in the bedroom doorway in her peach-coloured nightie and blocked his way. She didn't marry a lazy man, she said, but look what she has now – everyone knows people who blame others are the laziest sons of bitches around, let alone men who point fingers at their own sons without even being close to understanding what it is to be a father. 'She calls him a cocksucker and kicks him and sits in the closet with the door closed. Didn't you know that?'

It can't be true. Kate has always called Lyle 'Mr Margoulis' and is too shy to have anything resembling a conversation with him, not that he ever tried overly hard.

Lyle gets off the bench. 'So I guess we're free now, eh?'

Letitia walks with him up the main path, the paved one opposite where she ran down this morning.

The cars are loud up top and it's good to hear a regular sound. 'Do you need a ride anywhere?' he says and even though she's shaking her head he keeps going: 'I mean, I don't have the car right here, it's a six, seven-block walk. But I can go get it.'

She's still shaking her head. 'Ever wonder why stuff happens?' she says. He shrugs and she shrugs back. 'I was supposed to write a test this morning. I wonder what he looked like.'

'Okay, well,' Lyle says. And he zips up his coat to show he's leaving, though it's even warmer up on the sidewalk. 'Letitia,' he says, feeling sly at being able to remember the name.

'It's Tish,' she says. She sticks out her hand. 'I'm glad I wasn't all by myself.'

Lyle pulls his hand out of his jacket pocket to meet hers.

Letitia goes east, same direction Lyle's going. Except he

doesn't. He turns right. A goodbye should have an end to it. Not that he's ever liked saying it. An ending is a thing that rolls around in the mind and pretends to make sense. Someone goes away and doesn't come back.

He could have insisted. She might have given in. They could have gone to the police station together. He sees them stopping for lunch at the house, him clanking bottles around in the fridge looking for black currant juice because she's probably never had it before and checking to see if there's any cottage cheese. That's one thing he's never understood – the girls being so keen on cottage cheese. Him trying to get her to eat one of the best dill pickles she'd ever taste and her shaking her head.

He can see her picking up Joan's doodads from the window sills, squirrels and the like, and understanding how long they've been married. He can see the girl looking at all the pictures of Jeffrey.

Jeffrey, who may be living in a basement apartment now or a farmhouse or a condo. Jeffrey, who may be playing dodge ball at recess this very moment, or copying the words *kite* and *bicycle* from the blackboard.

When Lyle gets home, he sits in his chair, but he can't sit and he can't stand and he's starving but doesn't want anything so he swigs down some vitamins with apple cider. That weight in his hand, the crinkle of plastic. Lyle wants to feel pure. He wants to pray or something stupid like that. He's going to have to take Gravol tonight to sleep. And even then he'll have to make himself think scientifically, about things like how cows have four stomachs and how there's never any talk of cancer of the gallbladder or the heart or the eyes.

Maybe what you're supposed to do when you find a corpse is shake yourself good and hard, get ready to take in such a big breath it's going to give you a bastard stitch in the side.

He decides to look for Jeffrey. Lyle has to find his grandson today, or else what was the point of finding the body? He puts his coat on, walks to a bank machine and takes out forty dollars. He gets change in the laundromat next door where it's warm and the walls are yellow and a couple of kids are playing checkers on the floor. Jeffrey would lie down on his belly right next to them, chin in hands, and give advice from the sidelines.

Some people have laundry hampers or baskets, but most people slide their clean, folded clothes into garbage bags and sling them over their shoulders before heading out. If Letitia had spent her morning here instead of going jogging, she would have had a normal day. They both would have.

Lyle's come up with a system, a long-range plan, where he'll try to find Kate through directory assistance and he's going to do it here at a pay phone instead of at home so Joan won't see the bill and get pissy. Jeffrey's been gone for going on eight months now and Lyle's plan is pretty much crazy because Kate's maiden name is Murphy – might as well be Smith. But he'll do it for at least a month, see what happens. If you try, at least you can tell yourself you're trying. The way the system goes, he'll pick two towns a day, one close by and one far away, say Ajax and Victoria, and he'll get the operators to give him the numbers.

Town number one is Brantford. Town two is Truro, Nova Scotia. Random picks – he has no idea where Kate is. She's not at her parents', and they've told Joan they haven't heard from Kate either. Brantford and Truro are good places to start, small enough so he can get through all the numbers fairly easily. There's a recording at the first number with a woman's voice saying, 'I'll get back to you *toute de suite*.' Not Kate's style. Besides, Lyle's not going to leave any messages. What would he say? I know you're hiding from us, but come out, come out wherever you are?

No, if he ever does get her on the phone, he's going to have to say *We love you* right off the top. If there's any chance of seeing

18

Jeffrey again, Lyle has to say it, even though he doesn't love Kate. Even though he could smack her for stealing Jeffrey away from him. He's pictured it, shaking her, shoving her into the corner.

But if she picks up, he'll have to pull something genuine out of himself that will maybe help make up for whatever it is that's wrong.

'I love you, I love you, I love you,' Lyle thinks as he dials. No one answers any of the calls. At the last number, in Truro, there's not even a human voice. Only the sound of a cuckoo clock before the machine starts recording.

He wants to see the girl again. Letitia would go all-out to find Jeffrey if he was missing from her life – she takes her responsibilities seriously. Letitia could have talked herself out of believing it was a body stuffed into that bag so unnaturally, forced into a crude fetal position. She could have told herself it was just boots and coats in there. She could have let the corpse stay in its plastic membrane, knowing someone else would find it eventually. She could have kept on running and not said a word to anyone, same way Kate did with Jeffrey.

In the ravine, there are still two police officers standing near the body spot, looking bored. Yellow tape is looped around tree trunks in something like an octagon. Lyle is halfway up the slope. He wants to know if the body was a male or a female. If it was a stabbing or a shooting or a strangulation. If it was done for money or out of spite. He sees a flapping neck, the doing of it, the knife coming out and someone actually pushing it into a tight, scared throat.

That bag in his hands. The lump of flesh he'd poked with the stick. Owned by a fellow who might have played soccer yesterday, or gotten a speeding ticket. Or a woman who might have just had her hair cut, or maybe had a cold. Maybe the last thing she did of her own free will was cough.

Lyle holds out a piece of paper to the officers. 'Would you give this to Sgt. Boland?'

It is a folded note asking Boland to ask Letitia to phone Lyle. Urgent, he'd written.

The officer nearest him holds out her hand, dubious, flaps open the note and reads it.

Lyle points to where the spot where the body was this morning. 'It's just that the girl is so young – we found the – she found the – well, my wife wants her to come for supper so we can make sure she's all right.'

Sometimes a lie comes out truer than you'd expect. Joan would want the girl to come to the house.

The officer doesn't say anything.

'So?' Lyle says. You have to let them know you're serious or they treat you like you're already in a home.

'I'll pass the note to Sgt. Boland. That's all I'm promising.'

'Wonderful,' Lyle says, although he'd only been planning to say 'thanks'.

His head is buzzing again so he turns around and goes down and sits on the same bench as before. Should've had a couple slices of cheese, an apple. What he's got a craving for though is broth, cup after cup, a big thermos of it. Good and salty and sweat-making but not so hot as to burn the tongue.

He'll go and get a bowl of soup on his way down to the police station to make his statement. He'll ask again while he's there about getting a message through to the girl.

Lyle will watch the newspapers and learn the name of the victim and go to the funeral. The corpse is somebody's son or daughter. From the heft, a young person – small and slim enough to be shoved into the bag. He wants to see the body in a state of respect, out of that bag, framed by buffed oak or pine. Lyle and Joan will sit toward the back of the church. The girl probably won't be there and probably won't call, but so long as you try.

Letitia had squeezed hard when she shook Lyle's hand goodbye, a firmness stemming more from confidence than friendliness. He'd felt like his own hand was tainted from touching the bag, and then there it was – warm skin on warm skin, just for that moment. In his mind, he sees the contrast – his fingers grey against hers, his thumb reaching almost to the top of her wrist. But when it happened what he'd actually looked at was her eyes, and the way they focused right back on his.

There's a lot to tell Joan. Tonight when she gets home from work, he's going to say these exact words: 'I want to run some things past you.' That'll make it sound casual so she won't get scared. It'll also make it so he has to keep going and tell her how good it's going to be when she retires next year and how all-alone he is just now.

❧ Itty Bitty Road ❧

I'm about to get us a drink, I'm just leaning in to order it when this guy next to me says, 'Careful there, love.' And I'm thinking if he says one more word to me, if he says boo, if he even sneezes, I'm going to tell him to fuck off. Because a) no little shit sniggers at me and b) I especially don't like this little shit's rat-pus teeth.

Beer is a buck, you can have any kind you like as long as it's Blue and as long as it's in a can. Drinks are a dollar a double, which is why me and Mitch always get rum and Pepsi. Like he says, get a beer and you're throwing fifty cents out the window.

Arsehole's eyes are still Velcroed on me while I wait, he's poking his buddies and his face is cracked with laughter, like he's proud of his tea-stained piss-stinking teeth or something. The bartender pushes my drinks over and when I reach for them he crooks his finger like he's got something important to tell me so I lean in and he screams in my ear, 'Haven't you read the sign?' And the boys are going ooga ooga like they're going to crap their pants.

I look up but I don't see it and then I look over and there it is: No Boobs on the Bar.

So yeah, welcome to the Bulldog Club, located in beautiful uptown Goose Bay, Labrador. Home away from bloody home for the Royal Air Force.

They have two clocks behind the bar, one on our time, one on Greenwich Mean. They drink a toast to the queen at midnight their time, and one to Diana at midnight local time. Mitch and I have only been here for the Di one. They turn down the music and three or four guys try to grab the microphone and whoever wins walks around with it mashed against his lips. The guy'll say stuff like, 'You fine, fine lady, you're wanting a real man, I think you're wanting a real man such as myself. Chuck's not a man, you need a good man, I think I could do you some good.' Sometimes it strings along for five minutes. The last line is always the same: the guy with the mike says, 'I love you, Di,' and everyone in the bar lifts their drink and says, 'I love you, Di.'

Mitch always says, 'I loathe you guys,' just before he drives his glass into mine.

But we like the place, me and Mitch. They play the Clash and they play Adam Ant. Which, as Mitch says, is something around here. Plus it's the only military club you can get signed into without dropping someone else's name. Anyway, they just sit around and say ya, ya, at the German club and drink this dark beer like they're fondling it. The fucking kooks are in love with this brown beer. At the Canadian club, the guys wear Mickey Mouse ties. At the Mac club, the Americans wear slitty little black leather ties, and Mitch has never explained why exactly, but he gets homicidal in there. Which is fine, because I'm not into silk shirts and pleated pants. Also, I'm engaged to Sammy and I'm not supposed to be into anything.

Mitch keeps saying, 'He'll never know,' like it's a big joke. Just because all the other guys around here are sharks doesn't mean Mitch is any different.

So we do the Dog. Ten bucks each, we're smashed and we still have cab money. You can't go wrong. There is that tooth thing, though. I figure something like half the Brits sucked bottles full of tar when they were babies. And those same guys are all short. They're also jokers. They don't believe you when you show them the engagement ring and tell them a big man is going to wedge his toe into their belly buttons and feel around for their spines.

'That's just a line,' they say. 'That's just a ring. All girls have rings.'

It's my grandma's engagement ring, she always wore it even

though my granddad left her and moved in with another chicky. Not much of a ring, really. Granddad never really did wet his pants for Grandma. She made me take it to keep the military boys away. I've had perfume that worked better. Sammy says there's a real ring coming. That's what he said, I'm only repeating it.

'So boobs on the bar means you have to buy a round,' Mitch says. Then he says, 'I guess with your build it's hard not to.'

I'm shaped like a coffee can. Not like Mitch is the Man from Glad or anything. His shirt is always untucked over his belly. Which feels okay when I slap my hand on it, my cold rum hand.

'Hey.'

'Who's carrying too much what?'

'Come on, it was a compliment. You're nicely laden.'

'What?'

'You're well-laden.'

'What?'

'Laden. L-A-D-E-N.'

'Oh. Yeah, and wouldn't you like to set my table.'

'Indeed I would.'

He talks like that. If he's talking about a court case he's covering, he'll say something like, 'The man thought his only choice was to steal the money. Sadly, he was wrong.' Or he'll say, 'It's a sombre sky, don't you think?'

Sammy's not like that. He talks the same as everyone else. Never shuts up, actually.

We're standing by the emergency exit and Mitch is smoking out the door. It's not too cold, it's springtime in Siberia. Lights are moving up and down the runway like a bunch of coal miners practising for a funeral or something.

'Innu,' Mitch says.

Every year they block the runway to try to stop the Allied Forces from doing their jet training. The military police are doing a sweep over the tarmac.

'Good,' he says, 'I need one more item for the paper.' Which is called *Big Land Weekly*. Mitch calls it *Big and Leaky*.

'Come on,' I say.

They're playing 'Anarchy in the UK'. I push Mitch ahead of me and when we get to the dance floor, he sticks his cigarette in his mouth and leans back like he's trying to get the smoke away from his eyes. I'm the only girl out there. The Brits are dancing boy-boy, they're slamming each other and running up behind each other's backs and giving themselves boosts. I see one guy's shoe go right between another guy's shoulder blades. Then they put on 'God Save the Queen'.

And more guys come up. The tall ones with good hair, the beauty boys.

And then an elbow or a knee or something tries to iron out my cheekbone.

Mitch is saying, 'Come on, Lucy,' but I'm tapping this red-head on the arm and poking harder each time. Finally Pumpkin Puke turns around and I whale him one in the stomach.

He squeezes my hands together and yells, 'What'd you do that for, love?'

I'm screaming, 'You don't fuck with me. You don't fuck with me.'

In the cab Mitch says, 'You know, you've really got an aggression problem there.'

'No kidding,' I say.

We're coming up to the base gate.

'That's something around here,' I say.

He starts laughing. He leans over and rubs my hair like I'm a goddamn dog.

'Quit that shit,' I say and he puts on a big pout, but from tonight on he calls me Scrapper.

I have a good mom, just so you'll know to leave her out of it. She does stuff with bleach that gets into the area of the mystical. And my dad – he checks his rabbit snares every day because otherwise they're going to suffer. A lot of people can't separate those two things about hunting, pain and death. Dad says the easy way to illustrate it would be to put wire around their necks for three days and see if the assholes aren't begging to be shot then.

Mom doesn't see any need for the kind of language he and I get on with, and I certainly wouldn't use it in front of my boss, would I?

No, Mom, I say. I wouldn't say that in front of Fuck Nuts.

I work for the town. Most of what I have to do is issue construction permits and get people to sign things. No wonder I'm violent.

So I don't know if you've figured it out yet, but Mitch is hurting for me. He wants me so bad I bet his lips are bruised from saying my name. It's no trouble to see the way he looks at me like he's trying to put the brakes on, but what's the point because the truck's going over the edge. And what do you think of his finger poking the left cheek of my ass like he was trying to make a dimple (while he was supposedly bending over to tie his shoe)?

'Uh. Sorry. Sorry.'

That's what he said. The man's afflicted. And if it weren't for Sammy (and okay, maybe Sammy's navigator, pretty good with directions I always say), I'd be getting dimples carved into my ass with the pointy end of a potato peeler, and I'd be showing Mitch my long johns. What with Sammy working in Yellowknife and all, I've had a hard time keeping my trapdoor shut.

I kissed Mitch one night. I thought he was awake, just lying back listening to Bob Dylan. Mitch is always saying I should stop talking for a while and just let the lyrics go through me, so this one night I sit there nice and quiet but I don't listen. To what? Like hey, I'm Bob, hey listen, hey hey hey hey, I'm Bob.

I'm so wise and I'm so big and I'm so fucking nothing.

What I'm doing is leaning in, sneaking over to Mitch's side of his couch and I'm looking at his face for a long time. I swear I can feel his cheek before my lips touch it. He doesn't open his eyes, so I go back to my corner.

But later on he says, 'When's Sammy coming back?'

So tell me that's a coincidence.

June is a weird month. Once I went into a dance at ten-thirty and there was still light in the sky and when I came out at two there was blue at the other end of the sky. If you don't go home until after four, you can't sleep unless you do hot knives.

I'm calling and calling Sammy, he's never home. Guess he's not sleeping much either. Better not be some bitch involved. She wouldn't look good with a face full of scabs. He wouldn't do that to me, I don't think. Although his dad was hard at it all the time, everyone knew that. Sammy, he'd rather go out to the cabin for a weekend than be ripping teddies off of me.

I miss him snoring in my ear. I miss how he tries to make me late for work by making me breakfast in bed and not letting me get into the shower until I've eaten every last hash brown. I miss how he gets mad at me when I let off and plow someone, even if it is a total asshole.

'I can't take much more,' I tell Mitch. 'A girl has stuff inside that'll bust if it doesn't get used.'

'Oh my, couldn't have that, could we? A strapping milkmaid like you.'

He's the only guy who's allowed to talk to me like that.

He says, 'I've been thinking about how I miss parkas. I want winter to come back fast. I do this thing when I'm waiting in a line-up at the Northern store or something where I pretend the women are all naked under their parkas, and I give them one long zip. One long, extremely mysterious zip.'

'Yeah, so. I want to have sex on a ski-doo.'

'Better still, on an ice-pan. A couple of sleeping bags, that'd be peachy.'

'Ever done it on a bus? That's pretty good too.'

'Um, no.'

Black spruce looks exactly the same all year long. Everything looks exactly the same all year long. Except sometimes it's snow in your face, and sometimes it's black flies. We're driving onto the base, going to a movie. The Arcturus theatre has this white parrot in the lobby. Its cage has shredded paper inside, straight from the Colonel's office, Mitch figures. Once some pieces were sticking out the sides and Mitch shoved them in his pockets. He always says, 'Tell me what you know. Tell me what you know, Pretty Polly.'

The bird's name is really Flummy. They say the only words it can say are 'caribou' and 'stew'. Flummy is kind of fucked-up and squawks during kisses and shoot-outs. Seeing as the movie is *Terminator 2*, the bird is having a bad night. So is Mitch. He isn't saying much when we get in his truck.

'We should have left,' he says. 'What possessed us to stay for that?'

I say, 'It was kind of bad but no point putting your balls in a noose or anything.'

Mitch looks like he wants to hit something.

'What's this?'

The base has all these back roads, places where people go berry-picking or take their dogs. We're at the intersection of one of them and Mitch wants to turn left but a big chain is swinging across the road, with a No Trespassing sign next to it.

Mitch turns around, drives some more, we hit another chain. He sits there with his foot on the brake, his head on the steering wheel.

'I just want to drive somewhere, Scrapper. All I ask is to go for a little drive.'

He looks so pathetic I want to squish him between my boobs.

'We could go to 'Striver.'

Which is local for North West River, and it's as far as you can go by paved road. I'm hoping he'll say no because I don't think driving for half an hour and then turning back is going to make him feel like a lottery winner. I can see the shit Bruce Springsteen would write if he lived here. 'Same Old Road.' 'Itty Bitty Road.' 'Same Old Itty Bitty Road.' In Goose Bay, there's one doughnut shop, a Greek restaurant, one traffic light, and the Catholic church is one of those pre-fab kits made out of corrugated metal. There's a section in the parking lot for ski-doos.

'Nah,' Mitch says, 'I've got an idea.'

A plane is going over. Commercial, not a fighter. They fly in daylight in pairs. There's enough of a glow in the sky the body shines like a light bulb in a fridge.

'Think it's going to Halifax?' he says.

'Fuck no. Chicago.'

'Beijing.'

'Panama City.'

'Lisbon.'

It's this little game we play all the time.

He starts the truck, smiles and waves at the guard at the main gate and says, 'Fuck you' between his teeth. In the Valley, we pick up some beers and drive onto the beach.

What I want to know is why does everyone in the entire world start twirling around and running in these big lunky circles when they're on beaches, even when they're pathetic beaches?

When we get tired, we squat down and drink some beer. We drink one at a time, passing it back and forth. I'm thinking Sammy, baby, why didn't you phone me, why didn't you phone because I'm maybe, possibly, yes, going to be a very bad girl tonight.

'Scrapper?'

'Yeah?'

'I'm cold.'

'I gotta piss.'

'So piss.'

'Where?'

'Surely you're not one of those girls, Scrapper.'

'Suck my plantar wart.'

I walk till I can't see him any more, only the red of his cigarette.

'Come here,' he says when I get back and he's pounding the sand beside him. He puts his arm around me.

'Guess that's a story, those gates,' he says. 'They're afraid of the Innu. It's going to be quite the summer. Quite a good summer.'

I tell him about Sammy that time. He's driving down to 'Striver, it's early winter, only about minus ten, and there's this guy hitchhiking at the halfway point. He doesn't have a coat on so Sammy pulls over and tells him he'll take him to Sheshatshiu. And everything's fine for a couple of minutes but then the guy starts talking and he's high on something. Not booze, Sammy says, he was talking too clear and fast, he just wasn't making sense. So Sammy says 'uh huh' a lot, to be polite.

All of a sudden the guy has both hands wrapped around Sammy's neck and he's not killing him but he's not hugging him either. Sammy doesn't know what to do. He's got a bag of chips and Sammy says, 'Hey buddy, you want some chips?' And the guy lets go of Sammy and starts porking and Sammy takes him home.

No fucking way I'd be all nice-like to that loser but Sammy gets all holy about Doing the Right Thing. Sometimes I figure I'm one of his projects too. I trust him best when he's drunk, then I know who he really is. Not very nice, and not too skanking worried about it. Which is me, that's my life every day. Except I have a couple of rules. I don't hit anyone wearing glasses and I don't even so much as yell at someone I respect. Because otherwise, where are you?

'Fucking Indians,' I say, 'they should put them somewhere and keep them there.'

'Jesus, that's enlightened.'

'They're ugly and lazy and they use everything they can until there's nothing left.'

'How can you say that? Do you know what it's like for them?'

'And they're fat and smelly and I'm tired of seeing them on TV.'

'Stop.'

'I live here, too. I'm not going to fucking stand by and let them eat fried chicken all the time and leave their stinking diapers everywhere. Not on my land, mister.'

'Shut up, Lucy.'

'What's the matter, gone native? Got a hard-on for some squaws?'

'Stop it.'

'You'll have ugly, greasy babies.'

'Stop it. Just stop. I'm not listening to this shit.'

'And they – '

'Will you stop it? STOP. Close your fucking filthy mouth.'

He doesn't have to go crazy like that. It's just a conversation.

We sit not looking at each other, not drinking beer. No arm cosy around me. My butt is grinding into the sand.

Finally he says, 'How's the job going, anyway? You never talk about it.'

'It's just one big joyride after another.'

He smiles a little.

'Scrapper.'

We sit a while longer. He puts his arm back around me, tight around my shoulders.

He says, 'Keep a secret?'

'Yeah, whatever.'

'I'm getting married as soon as I get transferred out and I'm exceedingly nervous.'

'That's wild. Congrats and all that shit.'

The next time we go to the Bulldog, I kick this idiot in the shins when he sticks his hand on my ass. I tell him he's lucky I'm in a good mood or he'd be written up in all the medical journals as the guy with a dick that goes in instead of out. Then I drag some schmuck home with me, it's not even midnight, they haven't done the toast to Di yet. I'm holding him by the sleeve and I take him over to where Mitch is standing.

'I'm splitting.'

'Okay.'

And then he leans in all concerned-looking and says in my ear, 'But what about Sammy?'

I say, 'Never mind the bollocks,' and we're out the door.

Sammy who? Hasn't phoned. Doesn't care. I smell bitch.

Mitch and I don't talk about these things. Except once he shows me a picture of his girlie-poo, she lives in Halifax. Put it this way, she doesn't look like me. Mitch says she plays flute and that he wishes she'd fatten up a bit.

His fucking cat. A leg-hold trap would be too good, if you could find one any more. Mitch thinks this cat is Marilyn Monroe in a litter box, calls the thing Bauble. The jeezly thing bites me whenever Mitch isn't looking, follows me into the bathroom, backs me up against the wall and chomps away at my ankle. And all I can do is stand there and tell myself to breathe. One time I had to beat it off with the toilet plunger.

You're probably thinking, what's a big-boned girl like me doing afraid of a stinking cat? First of all, you've never met Bauble. Second, I bet you have your own thing, like moths or cliffs or ladybugs.

Okay, if you're afraid of ladybugs, you're an asshole. But everything else counts.

'Mitch?' I say. I'm sitting in this old rocker with two spindles crunching into my spine and I'm watching him rub the cat, which is vacuum-sealed to his chest and Mitch is KISSING the cat and I'm watching these long white hairs float around the room and the rocking chair doesn't even move right because of the carpet.

'How come we never go to my place?'

'Because you're a slob. And your music sucks.'

He goes back at Bauble. I keep trying to make the rocking chair go. A lot of times we don't talk much, but I know he wants me there. After a while, Flea-Whore jumps down.

Mitch says, 'If we lived in say, Philadelphia, and somehow we'd been introduced to each other, do you think we'd associate?'

'Associate?'

'Yeah, hang out. Do this.'

'Yeah.'

'We would?'

'Yeah.'

'Really? Really truly?'

'We're meant to be stuck in some shithole somewhere together.'

'I don't know. In fact, I can say with some assurance that anywhere else except here, I would not talk to you. I'd be scared of you, Scrapper. I probably wouldn't even like you.'

'Yeah, I'd be too much for you. I'd be too fucking real for you.'

'But you are – how shall we say – a diamond in the rough. That's kind of what you are, at least to me.'

I don't say anything. Sometimes the smartest way to get someone to yap the goods is to shut up and stare.

'Which is to say although I hate this place, at least you're here. Despite your tendency to commit assault and battery on a regular basis.'

I see the pillow coming just before it hits my head. Nobody throws shit at me and lives. I pin him on the couch.

'I'm going to give you a wedgie for that, you bastard.'

He laughs so much I lose my strength. And he pushes me off when I don't expect it so I land on the floor doing a form of the splits. He looks down at me from the couch, still laughing.

He says, 'I'd never ever talk to you. Even if you asked me what time it was. I'd just keep walking.'

❧ Fascia ❧

'You've splayed me,' Sandra says, arms and legs forming an X. 'I am absolutely splayed.'

And Misha knows what she means. Just getting to the fridge is hard. If he needed to make a fist, he'd feel weak. But he doesn't try – doesn't want even that slight frustration.

They are honeymooning in their own apartment.

He imagines he's been gutted. He's a fish and he's stopped flopping, eyes fixed in their jelly. But he's still a tiny bit alive. His lips work stupidly.

Because Sandra's limbs claim most of the bed, Misha's on his side, head propped on an open hand. It's hard to push his jaw open and talk with all that weight bearing down on his wrist, but he does. 'We're at this store in Listowel where they sell sports stuff second hand. I'm in the back corner trying on everything as fast as I can. Dad's wearing his sweater with the buffalo head on the back and looking around, coming over and leaning into my ear and saying, "When are you going to cut your hair? Ever done a push-up? Hurry up, Daisy." I pull some hockey pants over my jeans and pull them right back down. I'm trying to go so fast.'

It's all the sex, Misha thinks; that's what makes him talk. He stings – his lips, his cock, the inside of his legs. His chin is sore. Sandra makes him shave because she's rubbed raw, too.

Sandra makes Misha sit up with her. She looks into his face. She pulls his ears hard. Misha pushes her hands away.

'Let me,' she says.

Misha shakes his head. 'I get to the skates he's picked out for me. My toes are so crimped I can hardly walk across the carpet, and he says to the clerk, "We'll take 'em." The clerk says, "I don't know, maybe you want a pair with some growing room, you know, get that much more use out of them." My dad says, "Leather's nice and stiff and I don't get why you're not so interested in my money here." He made me put on the skates in the car to stretch the leather. The one time I ever cried when he pulled a stunt like that he was happy because he could call me a faggot all the way home.'

Sandra grabs his T-shirt from beside the bed to wipe her eyes. He tries to put his arms around her, but she keeps putting hers over his, and finally he gives up. They fall asleep but don't move again for a long time after their eyes open. She asks him what he's thinking about.

'How you're lucky to have such straight teeth.'

He doesn't tell her anything else. There's nothing he's got this big urge to repeat. His dad's been dead long enough to make everything better.

On his birthday, Sandra hands him a gift certificate for something called Rolfing.

'It's supposed to really fucking hurt,' she says. They're on the futon, lolling around to avoid making Sunday breakfast.

She pulls down his Fruit of the Looms and says, 'It'll be good for you. Or maybe I'm wrong as usual?' She licks him. 'Am I wrong again, baby?'

The Rolfing guy's name is Joe, and he's very short. He explains Rolfing to Misha in terminologies that include *lateral compensation* and *energizing fascial restrictions* and asks Misha if he has any questions.

'Is it going to hurt?'

Joe takes Misha's arm and says the best thing to do is just show him. Joe digs his thumbs into Misha's forearm and just about rips apart the muscles.

'It's like so. Can you handle that? And don't feel any pressure here, because it's not exactly for everyone.'

Crumbs on the kitchen linoleum pressing into Misha's cheek. His arms locked in a full nelson. *What's the matter, can't take it?*

'No worries,' Misha says.

Sandra is belly-down on the couch, reading. Just taking his coat off, he feels that arm burning.

'So?'

'We just consulted this time.'

'No body work?'

'Remind me again why I'm doing this?'

'For you to be home in your body.'

'I eat bacon.'

'So?'

'That's who I am. I eat bacon.'

'Mainly it's for your back, baby. To get your back fixed up.'

The first session, Friday after work, is mostly on his legs. Some of it's a cold but burning pain that doesn't actually hurt much because of the cold feeling; some of it goes right to his stomach, just like a blister that keeps getting rubbed. Joe uses his elbows to get right in there. It hurts so much a couple of times he wants to ask Joe to stop. But just as he's about to – *scaredy-boy* – Joe moves to another spot.

Joe is surprised by how well Misha takes it, says some of his patients yowl and some don't come back. He actually says that word, *yowl*.

Rolfing is about fascia. Joe says it's that white membrane you see on raw chicken after the skin's pulled off. Joe says fascia is an envelope that holds the body in shape. It toughens over time because of stress and bad posture and clamps the body into a smaller space. Joe says all he's doing is coaxing apart the fascia. Misha says he'd hate to see Joe being forceful, but Joe doesn't laugh.

The next day Misha wants to stay in bed. His legs ache, and that's just the physical part. His head hurts like he's just broken up with someone.

By three o'clock, Sandra's irritable. She clicks off the golf and tells him to get up and come with her to get groceries.

'I'm learning how to be in my body,' he teases her.

'Come on, baby, I mean it.'

'But I feel really weird.'

'I'm not doing all the chores by myself.'

'Can I tell you something? About before?'

Sandra says of course and lies down on top of the covers.

'This one's my first memory. I'm on Mom's shoulder staring at her hair, which she must have had permed and dyed because it's wavy and red. And then there's sun in my eyes, I'm looking out the living-room window and Mom's rocking me in the chair; I'm warm as if we've been there all morning. My sister Shelly flashes past the window. Then she's inside right in front of the rocking chair, crying.

'I asked Mom about it a few years ago, and she said probably it was the bullies. Now when I see Shelly there she has her fists knotted. There's a bloody hole in one of her stockings, and you can see where the other knee has already been darned. But I don't know if that's how it really was.'

Two Fridays later, Joe sticks his hands right underneath Misha's ribcage and declares a major release has happened. He tells Misha that sometimes emotional detoxing follows, because the liver sits on the right side under the ribs, and because someone digging around in there could make Misha feel vulnerable.

'Give me some eggs and hashbrowns and I can get through anything,' Misha says. Joe opens his mouth but says nothing.

Next day, Misha's fine. 'I'm really breathing now,' he says to Sandra, putting her hand on his diaphragm.

'Are you sore again?'

He's not that bad, but he wants to hang out in bed again so he says yes. Sandra waits. He waves her over, makes her get under the blankets so he can spoon her. He tells her about the first time he had sex (Rosemary Gerber with her tennis skirt on, the heels of her runners digging into his calves, a musty smell in the orange carpet behind her father's padded vinyl bar). He'd wanted to cry. Somebody should have told him that while he was still on top of Rosemary, he'd slap the mini-fridge to express his wonder, and then feel so invincible he'd fall in love with the smarting sensation and almost kiss it, except Rosemary's lips would get there first.

'Which hand?' Sandra says.

When he holds it up she rubs her nose in circles on his palm before kissing it, and while she's doing that he rubs her clit and puts a finger inside her the way she likes. He tries to pull her on top but she wants the bottom. She leaves her T-shirt on, and rests the soles of her feet on his calves, which makes it so they both come fast.

'I think this Rolfing is a good thing,' he says later. 'I feel lighter.'

'I'd call it lazier,' Sandra says. She's come back to the bedroom for her sneakers. 'So don't go crazy vacuuming,' she says, 'or anything nice like that to surprise me.'

The whole time she's gone, he lies with both hands on his ribs, feeling the air pushing up and out.

As he speaks, Misha's index finger runs laps around his lips, which feel soft, soft as Sandra's. This is what it feels like to talk.

Misha tells Sandra about the time his family took the ferry to Flowerpot Island in Georgian Bay, which looks exactly like a stone flowerpot that has trees planted in it. They took the trail up and around the rim and everything was fine until Misha, who was maybe five, didn't see a break in the planking. There was a shock as the board rammed his armpits. It happened so fast he didn't say anything, just swung for a bit, nothing under his legs except a couple hundred feet of air and a few yards of rock under that. Then he felt a new pain, his father pulling him up and dusting him off. His parents didn't say anything either. But his father lifted him again, propped him against the rock face, took his picture right away. They told Shelly to sit on the steps and not to move and that, no, she couldn't be in this snap, maybe later.

'He loved you,' Sandra says.

'That's what I'm telling you, he loved me.' He feels stupid saying it, but it bugs him she said it first. Even though he wasn't going to.

Seven treatments, and Misha's back is way better. No more seizing up when he wakes. Fewer headaches.

Not that it's come for free.

'I'm starting a catalogue of pain,' he tells Joe. 'There's the regular stuff, minor acute pain, the extremely foreign and unnatural kind that resonates; there's familiar but aggravating pain –'

'Pins-and-needles pain, deep pressure pain, keep-going-you're-an-inch-from-being-free pain, knife-down-the-ligament pain.'

Misha snorts, assuming Joe is having fun with it.

But Joe's face is even. 'As long as it has a purpose. As long as there's not just more and more, and you're sitting there wondering why.'

'Do you do this to kids?'

Joe says they don't need it.

When Misha walks, his head is up, shoulders down. In the mirror, his slouch hump has straightened. His gut doesn't stick out.

He doesn't stay in bed every other Saturday any more. After

a session, he's still stiff, but it's not a soreness that makes him feel like some old man.

The second-last session, Joe says he'd like to mention a couple of things. One, his sister passed on yesterday and, two, he's going to have to do some work inside Misha's mouth.

'Jesus, I'm sorry.'

But Joe makes a small smile. 'No worries. I'm not going to do the wailing-flailing thing. It was cancer, and now she's free, and I'm happy for her.'

Joe tells Misha he took his sister to Vegas before she died, like she'd wanted. 'She won two hundred bucks, and she wouldn't even buy me a beer. She was saving to buy a dress.'

This whole time, Joe's been doing his routine back and neck work. Misha can't think what to say. Anything he says might make Joe cry, and Joe doesn't want to cry.

'Oh my God.'

'What?'

'Here I am, and you probably want to go home. What an asshole.'

But Joe says it's okay, he wants to work. He says the only thing he's stuck on is whether he should go to the gym after, or run. Misha says run, definitely. Joe asks him if he has a sister. Yeah, he says. But he says nothing else about Shelly because he's still got her.

Joe's digging into the weak spots above his hips. Misha breathes into the pain and pictures it catching fire as he exhales.

Joe snaps on a pair of gloves. 'Okay, buddy, open up.'

Joe's finger cuts strings of tension that run along the outside pocket of Misha's gums. When his wisdom teeth started coming in, it hurt in the same irritating way. A voice in his head believes there would be real pleasure in biting down. Misha feels he's going to do it no matter how much he tells himself not to.

He takes Joe's hand in both of his and pulls, wipes the spit from his mouth.

Joe says, 'What's going on?'

Did you just say something?

Misha is silent.

Joe wrestles the gloves off. 'Come on, tell me what's going on.'

Misha can't make himself open his mouth. His heart's going like after a nightmare.

'Are you okay?'

Misha still can't talk.

Joe says probably he shouldn't have mentioned his sister like that.

'I just needed you to stop.'

Joe gives Misha a take-it-easy punch on the shoulder and walks out the door.

Misha is in the leather recliner when Sandra unlocks the door. He's crying.

'Baby?'

'I'm thinking about my sister and those holes in her stockings, and it's killing me to think about her knees being scabby all the time, and no one to help her.'

'Let go,' Sandra says. 'Just let go.'

Let it all hang out, dog breath, like you always do.

'I never got to say I hate him. I fucking hate you, cocksucker.'

'It's okay, it's okay.'

'I just needed him to help me, and I never said that to him.'

'Say it to me. Just say it to me.'

'Stop trying to fix me all the time.'

She pushes him away. Her gaze moves down to the floor and stays there. She starts shivering. After a while he tries to put a hand on her shoulder. She dodges it and runs to the bathroom, starts filling the tub. Misha tries turning the door handle very slowly so she won't notice, but it's locked.

In the morning, she won't roll over.

'I want you to know how it ended,' he says to her back. 'Because in a lot of ways it was the best thing that ever happened to me.'

Sandra doesn't move. Misha tells her about his father in the hospital, one side paralysed, Frankenstein stitches purpling his forehead, saying, 'I'm two for two with you kids, and I don't know why.' The weight of that line made them giddy – Misha and Shelly and their father mimicking their old dentist, Dr Watton, who had whistling dentures and a habit of saying 'shubshequently', all three of them saying it again and again, the *sh* sounds more and more drawn out.

'My father walked that night,' Misha says, 'and the nurse said it was a miracle. He asked for help, and two orderlies came and he took a few steps with them. Shelly and I were staying at this hostel for people with sick relatives. I remember we had a fight that night over the beds in the room we had to share. One had a wooden platform and was suspended from the ceiling on chains so it would swing. What bothered Shelly was that it was covered in fur hides. Both of us tried to make dibs on the regular bed that had an old-fashioned spread, you know, those kind your mom has.'

'Chenille,' Sandra says.

'Yes. Shelly says, "I'm oldest, and it's my call, and no fucking way am I sleeping with dead things on me." I'm not liking the idea either. I say there's nothing wrong with the big bed and sit at the foot to prove it, and the thing moves and bashes the wall. It's really loud and, sure enough, there are a couple of dents in the wall, and we wait for someone to tap on the door but no one does. We go crazy laughing because here's our dad in the hospital, and here's this swinging goat-hide bed that me and Shelly would have killed for when we were little.

'The woman who owns the house wakes us in the morning, says there's a call. The phone's in the hallway, so I go. It's my stepmom. Dad's gone. Back in the room Shelly's sitting up in the normal bed, and I start to say something, and she just says, "Was anyone with him?"

'When I go for coffee, there's a man in the kitchen whose thirty-two-year-old son is having heart surgery later in the morning, and he asks how my dad is, and I don't even think to lie to him. I can still see his face.

'We meet my stepmom at the hospital and walk to some sort of boardroom through the lobby where everyone's staring. Why they don't have a special entrance for people who just got the call, I don't know. This young nurse comes in, and she's crying, too, says she was the last to see Dad, that he pressed the buzzer at 4 a.m. for the bedpan. He made a joke about playing hide-and-seek with her – which was supposed to be funny because he couldn't move – and when she came back she couldn't find his pulse.

'The surgeon pops his head in the room, just his head. All I can think is his brain's making this quick appearance to explain about dad's brain. He says they'll do an autopsy, but he has to assume that a filament of the tumour wrapped around something fundamental. It would have been painless, he says. He's sorry.

'My stepmom says, "Let's get breakfast." And we do. That's what you do when someone dies. You eat. You sleep. But you're heavy. Everything is heavy. Like a fork. You try to pick up a fork and you think, shit, I don't know if this is going to work.'

Sandra has turned over and is watching him.

'The night after the funeral – it's my last before I fly home – Shelly says, "So, did we have a dad there for twenty-four hours?" I say maybe longer. He knew he was two-for-two and he knew he was a lucky bastard. Same way I am with you.'

'Yup,' says Sandra, pinching his ass. 'So you're saying you loved him.'

'I'm saying let's get out of the house for a while.' But he stays in bed while Sandra gets dressed. He listens to the coffee maker burping.

When she comes back, he's sitting on the end of the bed, very tall the way Joe showed him, thighs sloping toward the floor, the arches of his feet pressing down and pushing up at the same time.

'Take my picture,' Misha says, 'while I've got it. Right now. Get the camera.'

So Beautiful the Firemen Would Cry

I started keeping my toothbrush in my underwear drawer after Beanie told me what she did to her last roommate. She wanted to make sure I understood it was a very unusual thing for her to do and that she'd been extremely provoked along the lines of her bitch ex-roommate being two months behind on the rent and always eating Beanie's butter and then swearing innocence. I appreciated having the context, but it's still a little uncomfortable knowing the person you're sharing an apartment with used to twirl their old roommate's toothbrush in the toilet twice every day – first thing in the morning, and also after Beanie's last pee at night.

When she told me about it, Beanie said I must think she was terrible and I said, no, I kind of understood. But really, all I could see was that toothbrush going into the toilet twice a day and into a mouth twice a day.

After that, I kept an old toothbrush as a decoy in the holder, just left it there and never used it. Sometimes it seemed a little damp, but I'd have to wash my hands four times to get rid of any germs after touching it so after a while I stopped checking. Also, suspicion on that level kills something inside you eventually, which is why I decided to cool it.

One time she almost caught me. I was in my robe, getting ready to crash. I was going to do one of those round-trips – you know, go to the kitchen for a glass of water and then to the bathroom to wash my face before crawling into bed. I'd set the non-decoy toothbrush down on the counter. Just then Beanie came home and stuck her head in the kitchen door to say hi. After that, I kept the toothbrush under my pillow, wrapped in Saran Wrap, because I thought she might come looking for it and the drawer was kind of obvious. But like I said, what's the point of living like that? After a couple of weeks, I made myself put it back in the bureau.

Most times Beanie was an excellent person to live with. We had all this stuff in common: both of us were new to Vancouver and couldn't really get a grip on the place, and both of us were single. But it was more than just the big stuff. Beanie's the only other person I've ever met who eats popcorn with a spoon. Also, she used to read Baba Yaga stories when she was a kid, just like I did. And, weirdest of all, we both had aunts in Bathurst, New Brunswick.

We used to clean together, if you can believe it. We liked that – music going, a pot of chai on the stove, everything in its place all shined up. We were forever rearranging the furniture because our living room was about six inches square and we were determined to find a way to make it look bigger. But even with a white slipcover on the couch and a lick of white paint, the place still looked like a storage closet with a couch in it. We did a lot of this stuff on Saturday nights because we didn't have any friends. That was the thing about the city we couldn't figure. People would chat to me at the bus stop, or at the very least smile. And at school – which is why I was in Vancouver – everyone was nice, nice, nice, but I'd still go home on the bus right after class. Beanie had the same problem, even though she worked in a futon store, which you'd think would be a cozy place to develop inter-employee relations.

Whoever got home first would cook and make enough for the other person. That was usually me, and then Beanie would do the dishes. It was pleasant, you know. Our dining room was really a little balcony that had been glassed in. We could feel squirrel holes under the linoleum, but if the rain stopped we could see the mountains. Once I saw a coyote on the grass out front, and then a couple of days later I saw a guy standing in that exact same spot, shooting up.

It was pretty safe where we lived, which was in the east end, near Commercial Drive, although there was a crack house right around the corner. One time when I walked past, a man pushed another man down the porch steps while a woman whipped the falling guy with a rope. The rule with that kind of situation in Vancouver is not to make eye contact, just keep looking straight ahead. But coming in from Fredericton like I did, it took a while to figure that out. I remember this crazy guy downtown on a Sunday when I was walking to the Stadium Skytrain station. I looked right at him because I didn't want him to think that I thought he was crazy and he came at me with his arm out and his hand in a fist and said, 'You want a punch, you ugly fucking cow?'

In a way, that was my welcome to Vancouver, because it happened right after I arrived. So it was good to have Beanie around. She'd come in from Toronto, but she was even more disturbed by the city than I was because she'd decided Vancouver was where she was going to spend the rest of her days. I was going back to Fredericton to do my Ph.D. in English so I could live with my parents and save money. Beanie was living her dream of being in a big city that had mountains and sushi and beaches and monkey trees. She thought Vancouver was ahead of its time. She was proud that to get home from work, she'd catch the bus in front of this fetish shop called Cabbages & Kinx and then she'd hop off right outside the women's sex shop on the Drive which had a mural featuring butt plugs and vibrators and dildos kind of doing a happy dance together (picture that in Fredericton!). But it did bother Beanie, going through the downtown eastside. She told me that once she saw a sixteen-year-old who looked like she should be eating strawberry shortcake and wearing headphones, but instead was rocking back and forth on the sidewalk in the rain, no coat.

You could see it surprised Beanie, the yucky things she saw in Vancouver. She came home one night and said she'd just walked past nine people begging on the Drive and hadn't given any of them anything. She wanted to know what it did to you inside to keep walking past them, what it would do to you after ten years. I said just fork out extra rent money and move to Kits, like everyone else. She said there were lots of street people in Toronto but that they weren't all so young and didn't shoot up right in front of you.

They didn't do that in Fredericton, either, since no one lives on the streets. Saturday market is about as exciting as the place gets, or maybe the first thaw on the river.

Beanie said she needed a break and that I did, too. We'd heard Bowen Island was a funky place. We decided to go on the next sunny or semi-sunny Sunday or Monday because those were Beanie's days off. But it was November. We counted eighteen straight days of rain, and then I said we'd better stop counting for our mental health.

So Beanie told me to wake her up early enough to call in sick on the next sunny day, and I said sure. But I was lying, because I have this thing which is something like a phobia about not waking people up. I don't know why, but it makes me feel sick. There were a couple of okay mornings where they said on the radio it would be fairly dry that day, but I didn't go and get Beanie because of what I already told you.

One morning – I think it was December by then – Beanie slapped my door and said, 'Let's do it.' It was eight-thirty and there was enough light coming in through my curtains that I could see the corners of my room for a change. I could smell bacon and coffee. She did my eggs over easy for me and said she'd already called work. It was a Thursday. I was supposed to hand in a paper on Robert Kroetsch that Monday coming and hadn't started on it, because that's the way I am. I said I couldn't go, but she got huffy and I remembered the toothbrush story and wondered if I should provoke her.

We took the bus to Horsehoe Bay, and everyone waiting was

in a good, good mood. A sunny day in Vancouver is kind of like a full moon in some other places: it sure changes people. The ferry ride was nice – short, but still we could see the coast mountains and also one stretch of water out past the islands where it's just pure Pacific.

Put a rain forest on an island in one of the rainiest spots in the rain forest zone, and you get Bowen Island. We got onto the hiking trail straight off, where the moss on the trees was unbelievably green. If it was a paint colour, I'd call it 'Spanky Leprechaun'. There were ferns the size of nightmares running alongside the trail, and ravens screaming from the trees instead of monkeys. Our sneakers went right down into the mud. It felt to me like a place that was so alive that it was almost choking itself. Even the dead stumps of trees kept growing – moss spilled right out of them.

I had an inclination to find a clearing and stay there, but Beanie loved the woods. 'Smell that?' she kept saying. 'I'd put a cabin exactly here.'

It started to rain pretty hard, which made me a little more inclined to like rain forests since all that greenery acts like a leaky umbrella. It was Beanie's idea to get off the trail and onto this road we could see running close by. She figured we could hitch-hike, or that at least it would be a shorter walk back to Snug Cove and the ferry terminal. It was a dirt road and it kept forking into other dirt roads, so I knew we were probably walking away from the ferry landing instead of toward it. We walked past someone's tipi, but it didn't seem like there was anybody home. Same with a yurt. We were pretty wet and cold, but all the hippie stuff made us giddy – I mean, you hear people talk about how loopy B.C. is, but you think it's an exaggeration. We decided some woman named Kiki lived in the tipi, and that a guy named Kurt had the yurt.

Then we came to another fork in the road, except this time there was a rope across it and a sign saying visitors were welcome as long as they didn't let the horses out. There was a little gold Buddha sitting on top of a tree trunk, and next to it was another sign, with an arrow underneath the word 'Labyrinth'.

So of course we ducked under the rope and followed the arrow. There were all these little plaster cherubs and gnomes along the sides of the path. They looked extra white against all the dank and green and they scared me. Beanie was loving it, though. 'We are adventuring,' she said, 'and I moved here exactly because deep inside I am an adventuring babe.'

The labyrinth was in a small meadow, which calmed me down a bit. Someone had painted all these rocks white and used them to make the design. We stepped inside and started going around and around.

It was one of those prayer mazes – you know, all paths lead to God. After maybe ten minutes, I stepped outside the rock border. Going around and around was just too boring, and also a lot of extra walking; I wanted to save my strength for figuring out where we were.

But Beanie kept going. She hopped along on one leg for a while and then switched to the other. 'Kiki's tipi,' she said. 'Kurt's yurt.'

We were both laughing. 'Hurry up,' I said.

When she got to the centre, she dropped down on her knees. 'Wow,' she said. 'Big whoop.' But she stayed there for a few minutes before getting up. 'That's better,' she said.

As soon as we got back to the road, a pick-up went by. We flagged it down and got a lift right down to the ferry dock. There was a boat waiting, too, but we decided to get some fish and chips and catch another sailing. Even with all the grease, I could feel the beer buzzing in my blood. It made me wish I was there with a real friend, not just a circumstantial one.

Beanie told me that when she'd sat there in the middle of the labyrinth, she heard the same word running around and around in her head. She figured it had been going around like that for a long time, like one of those whirligig lawn ornaments that look like the guy's legs are moving because the winds spins them around.

My socks were wet and the pub was cold. 'Come on,' I said, 'we've got four minutes to get down there if we're going to get the next ferry.'

'I don't feel like rushing,' she said. 'I'm too full to run.'

I decided it was her call, since the whole trip was her idea.

'So, anyway, yeah, this word was *trust*, that's what was going around and around in there and I wasn't hearing it, you know?'

'Like literally? An actual word being said out loud in your head?'

'So I'm thinking I should tell you this thing which I've never told anyone.'

I didn't want to hear it. No matter what she said, it was going to affect me. Like that toothbrush story, only this one would be bigger, obviously. And it didn't matter what she said – whether she was pregnant or had HIV or got fired or was coming out of the closet – it was going to change my life.

She told me she'd tried to do herself in about three months before moving to Vancouver. She loved this guy Todd and they lived together but then he came home one night and said it wasn't working but that they'd be friends forever, wouldn't they? And she found out where he was and started phone-stalking him and then he got unlisted so she took some pills and put on this dark green silk nightgown number with a V-neck and lace straps and got into bed with the pillows just so and her hair just so because she wanted to look so beautiful the firemen would cry when they had to come and put her body on the stretcher.

But she barfed up the pills and didn't even go to the doctor's the next day because it only felt like a really bad hangover. She

didn't tell anyone, even though she had a roommate, the toothbrush one.

'So, you know, how's everything going now?' I said after
she'd gotten into the mechanics of suicide for a while and how
hard it is to die because your body wants to live no matter how
crap-plugged your mind is.

She said not to worry, that she felt great. That she was making all these little steps forward and that she knew Vancouver
would be really good for her once she got used to it.

I asked if she'd done the counselling thing and she told me
she didn't believe in stirring up the pot when it wasn't necessary and that she knew first-hand from when she was fourteen
and her mom sent her to a shrink that counsellors like to keep
everything edgy because it's more interesting for them. 'I mean,
you must know about that,' she said.

I told her I'd never gone to a professional.

'But you've tried the other solution, right? Everyone has at
some point.'

I've always kind of liked being alive, but I didn't want to say
that. 'I've had some crappy times.'

'So how?'

'Huh?'

'Which way did you try?'

I could see this excitement on her face as she waited for me
to answer. 'You've never?'

I shook my head.

'Wow,' she said, 'you're a little weird.'

After that I worried for about a month. I kept thinking that
Beanie was dead in her room, with the blankets cuffed nicely,
her whole torso propped up on pillows, her hands folded, her
skin damp and cold under that green nightdress.

Then Beanie met Frank. He had these eyes that could knock
you over. She was happy, all right. They went out to the

Railway Club and the WISE hall and to the tapas bar on the Drive where this band played funky flamenco music. She sewed herself a couple of sarong skirts out of batik fabric and wore them with a little white blouse tied in a knot at her belly button. She laughed a lot.

I was only jealous maybe ten or fifteen times, right at the beginning. I just felt kind of ugly and lonely, although it's not like I wanted Frank. He worked as a hand on a tugboat and I always knew if he was over as soon as I unlocked the door to the apartment because I'd either smell his sweat if he'd just gotten off shift or his Lysol-strength cologne if he was taking Beanie out somewhere. He said he figured he and Beanie were destined for each other, what with their names being Frank and Beanie, which he said you could boil down to Weenie and Beanie. 'Get it?' he'd say. 'Boil down. Get it?'

When Frank was stoned, he was useless. 'What time are we going again?' he'd yell out to Beanie, who would plant him in the living room while she got ready in her room.

'I said, we'll leave at nine-thirty.'

'Oh,' he'd say. Then after a few minutes, 'What time did you say, hon?'

He'd do that lying on the couch with his shoes planted straight down on the slipcover. Sometimes he'd fall asleep and would snore, which made me want to scream since I'd be in the kitchen maybe seven feet away trying to cook something for myself. What really pissed me off was that I'd actually try not to make much noise, because of how I am about waking people up. But one night I dropped a can of tomatoes on the floor on purpose. That gave him a jolt, all right. His feet flew off the couch and landed on the floor. I felt so bad I said, 'Sorry,' and then hated myself for being weak.

Each time Frank came over, he stayed longer. After about three weeks it was like he lived there. I came home one after-noon, and he had this jigsaw puzzle spread out on the dining-room table. It was supposed to be Van Gogh's self-portrait. Frank said he got it at Value Village and that he was going to put it together and glue it to some cardboard backing and then hang it on the wall. He said his friends would be impressed to see famous artwork at his place. But the thing was a bugger because each piece of the puzzle had these grids with tiny photographs of trucks and birds and stuff inside, to make it that much harder to do.

That jigsaw puzzle stayed on the table, which really was my table, for a week, about one-tenth done. I ate in my bedroom that whole time and thought about how good life would be without Frankenstein. What I did, finally, was vacuum every single stupid piece of that puzzle off the table. My alibi was going to be that I'd spilled a bowl of chicken noodle soup over the pieces by accident.

But I never got my chance – Frank disappeared. No phone call, no note, no nothing. At first Beanie was furious and then she got all worried that he'd drowned off the tug. Then she started crying all the time. I mean, all the time. She still went to work, so that was a good sign. But I'd call her for supper and she wouldn't come out of her room. I even made manicotti one night because she was wild for it, but she said sorry, she wasn't hungry. At night, I could hear her blowing her nose.

That Saturday when she came in from the Futon Factory, I caught her in the hallway before she could slide into her room. 'You okay?' I said.

She thought for a long time. Then she said, 'As well as can be expected.'

'Want a hug or anything?'

She shook her head and took a couple of steps toward her room. 'Come on,' I said, and I gave her a geeky hug that she twirled right out of.

'Don't worry, I'm not mental,' she said before she closed her door. 'In fact, I'm very clear at the moment.'

That really scared me. You get really calm just before you do it, right? I almost called one of those hotlines, but I decided to keep monitoring for the next couple of days.

On her days off, Sunday and Monday, she was a shut-in. But I could hear her clearing her throat or walking out to the bathroom. I put a jug of water outside her door and a glass but I didn't knock in case she was sleeping. When I came back from the supermarket, they were gone. So I made a cheese sandwich and left that out there.

I got up really late on Tuesday because I'd forced myself to make some headway on my paper on Ondaatje's *Running in the Family*. It was such a good read I hated to mess it up with an essay. Anyway, half the sandwich was gone. I didn't know if Beanie was at work or not.

When I got back from class, the half-sandwich was still there. It was 6:30 p.m. I took the plate away and there was no light coming through the crack in the door. I had to do something. By 9:30, I knew she was dead and I was pretty sure I was going to be sick. I was wondering if I could touch her but I knew I couldn't – I've never touched a dead thing.

I put the bottom of my sweatshirt over her doorknob so I wouldn't leave any prints that would lead the cops to believe it was murder. I kept my hand on the doorknob for a long time. Finally, I started pushing the door open.

'Beanie?' I called. 'Lucinda?' Which was her real name but she didn't like it because it reminded her of her childhood. 'Beans? You have to get up.'

Nothing. I stood really still and after a while I could hear her breathe. I wanted her to sit up on her own, without saying another word. I don't know why it bothers me so much, waking people up. It scares me the same way all that swamp on Bowen Island scared me. But I had to do it – Beanie needed help, and I was going to make her go through her address book and pick out three people and make her promise to talk to them about what Frank did.

I went over to her bed and put my hand on her cheek, really slowly. Her legs slid around a bit and I could see her eyes open.

'I'm sorry I touched you and I'm sorry I woke you up.' These slider tears were dropping right out of me, the kind that wet your whole face and roll under your chin.

'Hey,' she said, patting my hand a couple times.

'Look at you,' I said. She'd been crying so much there was hardly any eyeball showing through all the puffiness. 'Do you have your plans, you know, made?'

She sat up then and told me she would never, ever do anything like that to me – understood?

I said, 'But your old roommate, she would have found you that time.'

'First of all, that was not a smart thing. And second, this is friends here, okay?'

That just busted me, and then she started in, too. After a while I said, 'You want me to pour you a bath?'

She nodded. 'I know, I know, I'm going to have to talk to someone. In a few weeks or something.'

I Ajaxed the tub for her and made sure to do a good job rinsing the grit out. I splashed my face with water in the sink and that's when I saw the decoy toothbrush. I grabbed it and put this careful, perfect line of toothpaste on it. And you know, I almost brushed my teeth. Except I couldn't. What I actually did was chuck that thing into the trash.

❧ The Dogs ❧

The first time Darlene sees Marbles, she can't even see her. Someone's put a baseball cap over the puppy and the ball cap is moving around on the floor like the puck from a Ouija board. Kendra pulls it away, and there is Marbles, white with black spots. Kendra shows her sister the bump on the pup's belly and says it's called a hernia and that it will require an operation to make the puppy's innards stay in. Kendra says Marbles is hers. And Marbles is moving with them from the city into the new house.

A while after they move into the big house by the creek, with the tire-truck swing and the riding lawn-mower, their dad brings home another puppy. This one is named Nutmeg and is twice as big as Marbles. Because their dad has asthma, the puppies stay in the summer kitchen. Its floor is covered in newspapers and shit. Darlene counts seventeen turds one day. A couple of times a week, her mother goes in with rubber gloves and a garbage bag.

A highway rolls across the front of their lawn, but the dogs are never tied up when they're outside. A truck pulverizes Nutmeg's hip, and she has to be put down. After Nutmeg, there is Zorro, black with a tan mask.

Kendra lets the dogs lick her ice-cream cones. The sisters lie down in Darlene's grass fort on the bank of the creek and throw raspberries to the fish. Kendra tells Darlene that if a man ever puts his hand this high up her thigh, she'll have to kick him in the nuts.

That fall, the dogs are moved to a shed that used to be a chicken coop. The girls let the dogs in the house when their parents are in town on a Friday night. They listen to their father sneeze when he gets home but they still go ahead and let the dogs in the next time. Darlene raids the storage bin inside the bench in the mud room, and carries a pile of toques, gloves and scarves over to the dogs' house. It is a huge pile, but no one ever notices. She even picks the burrs out of the wool before she brings the offering to the dogs. They lick and wag like they always do, and she can't tell how cold they are.

School nights, the dogs blast down the banks of the creek just ahead of the girls' toboggan, which makes Kendra scream and cover her eyes. The dogs sniff her face when she falls down trying to shovel off a pond in the back field one Saturday. They're so short they bounce from boot-print to boot-print to get through the snow. Darlene watches Marbles chew frozen shit, her dewlaps pulled back.

Kendra puts boiling water in their kibble so that it will still be warm by the time she gets it to their pen. The dogs only go there at night. Otherwise, they wander around the property. Darlene has a special whistle for the dogs. Free-frew. Free-free-free-frew. Free-free-free-free-free. Her dad says he's seen both dogs cross the highway and that the girls have got to keep them closer in.

Kendra hates high school. Always has, always will. Their mom says she thought the move would be good, that farm kids would make good friends. Kendra says they haven't read *Siddhartha*. Plus which they draw tiny hearts instead of dotting their i's.

Darlene can't get her crocheted bookworm to curl, and her home-ec teacher finds it tricky to explain to a left-hander. Miss Dunfield has a Sucrets box full of google-eyes, in varying sizes. Girls can't take shop. On the bus home, the boys show off what they've made. They give their mothers chip bowls made out of melted sheets of blue plastic.

When the slush is gone, Marbles has four black-and-white puppies. Zorro has nine; some are black and some are tan. The dogs get to move back into the summer kitchen during this time. Darlene's dad finds homes for all of them with the kids at his school. He teaches grade seven and eight science and history in town. His classroom has cages with gerbils and mice and a snake and a lizard and guinea pigs, all donated by parents. He brings home two guinea pigs for the summer and puts them out on the lawn in a chicken-wire cage so that they can eat the grass. The dogs find a way to paw open the door. There is white and brown fur all over the lawn for a couple of days.

In the fall, Kendra goes to George Brown College to study graphic arts, which means Darlene gets to go with her mother to the weekly film club showings in town, and to any classical recitals that swing through.

Darlene knows every word of Kendra's diaries, which are hidden on the top shelf of her wardrobe, underneath her sweaters. Kendra believes nature is divine. She keeps her letters in a manila envelope taped underneath the pencil drawer in her desk. Mostly they're letters she's decided not to send. Many are to Farley Mowat, some are to Herman Hesse.

Kendra calls on Sunday evenings and their mom hogs all of the time on the phone. Kendra comes back for Christmas and tries to get the dogs moved into the summer kitchen. It's so cold out, she says. But their dad says what about the fleas. And also what about his asthma – and don't think he's about to start coming in the front door instead and tracking snow through the hall.

It's Darlene's job to take the food to the dogs. The path is hard to see in the dark, and she shivers. When her parents go into town on the weekend, Darlene lets the dogs stay in the house so that she won't be all alone. One night, she's too sleepy to put them back out so she pets them under the covers. The plan is that she'll sneak them out in the morning. But both dogs bark and run downstairs when they hear the car in the drive. Darlene pretends to be asleep when her mother comes upstairs and stops at her door, looking in.

The next time the dogs are inside, Darlene catches Zorro licking something inside her parents' room. It's a little glass that is sticky and smells like almond liqueur, her mother's favourite drink. It must have been under the bed. Now it has short black hairs stuck around the rim. The bottle is in the drawer where her mother keeps her T-shirts. Sometimes it's crème de menthe.

Darlene does not skate or toboggan without her sister around. The dogs come wagging when she walks down the drive from the school bus. She goes inside and reads, or watches reruns of 'Hogan's Heroes'. Her mother also has an expectation that she'll start sharing the cooking. Once a week, Darlene makes chili, scraping browned hamburger off the frozen slab in the pot, and squishing the canned tomatoes with a wooden spoon. Also, Darlene has to make her own lunch now, she's old enough. Her dad's already out the door before she gets dressed, and her mom doesn't want to get up in the mornings anymore. Sometimes Darlene runs some mayonnaise over the bread and puts a cheese slice in the middle. But mostly she doesn't take any food to school. The other kids have thermoses full of tomato soup and turkey stew. Their sandwiches have tuna, or smoked ham and cheese and lettuce. They have Baggies full of cut celery and carrots. They have iced cupcakes and oatmeal cookies. Darlene tries to wrap both hands around her brown-bread sandwich while she's eating so that no one can see it. Or she says uh-oh, she forgot her lunch again, and the girls all share what they have with her.

Once, on a Saturday, Darlene and her mother go to a matinee, and stop for apple pie and ice cream before coming home.

Kendra has won a scholarship for next year. And she's going to stay in Toronto over the summer and babysit for one of her instructors, who will give her free room in return. She comes home for Easter and for the twenty-fourth of May weekend. She looks very pretty in the smock-top one of her new friends gave her. She describes a bonfire at Cherry Beach, and talks a lot about a boy named Sven.

Kendra and Darlene set out for a walk in the back field but it's a swamp from all the rain. They can't see any white on Marbles. When they go inside, Darlene shows Kendra the bottle in their mother's drawer.

'Holy shit,' Kendra says.

She gives Darlene a mini-skirt she found at the coolest Sally Ann ever, on Queen Street. When she saw it, right away she knew it would fit. She has lipstick, too, if Darlene wants to try. Their mom has a rule that you have to be sixteen before you can wear black clothing, mascara or lipstick. Darlene worries that her mother will see how red her lips are from wiping it off.

One day after Kendra leaves, their dad goes through the pantry and the linen closet and the bathroom cupboards and he says to Darlene, 'Where is it?'

Darlene follows him through the house. 'What are you looking for, Dad?'

'Your sister told me what to look for,' he says. 'You know what it is.'

Darlene shakes her head and says, 'What's wrong, Daddy?'

He says, 'Your mother should never be left alone during the day.'

She takes him to the bedroom and shows him what she showed Kendra. But there are only clothes in her mother's drawer, folded sensibly. Her father says he's already looked there.

He gets the charcoal fired up a couple of times a week, and Darlene and her parents eat at the picnic table. The dogs sit and wait for pieces of fat to be thrown their way.

Darlene's dad says they should go to Lion's Head Park.

Darlene's mom says she doesn't want to.

They go the next week, and almost drown when some white-caps come up out of the blue when they're canoeing in

Georgian Bay. Darlene sits in the middle with the dogs, and her parents paddle.

'I think you earned a drink, Linda,' Darlene's dad says that night.

Her mom says, 'I was pulling as hard as I could and we weren't getting anywhere. Isn't is funny to think here we are, and Kendra and Sven are probably at a movie right now? I hope they're at a movie and not a party.'

The dogs sleep on pieces of foam rubber in the back of the station wagon during the camping trip. They get in trouble for not barking when someone tries to break into the car. Darlene's mom hears it happening and the man runs away when she screams from inside the tent.

The thunderstorms stop and it's time to go back to school. The other girls have bras and Midol, and the boys want to play truth-dare-double-dare-triple-dare-or-repeat with them.

At suppertime, Darlene's dad updates them on the progress of the film his after-school club is making, where it looks like student after student is jumping out of the same locker. 'The eye likes to be tricked,' her dad says. 'It invites it.'

Darlene's mom is planning a Mexican fiesta. She has been working on the piñata while Darlene and her dad are at their classes. She was going to make it in the shape of a cat but that didn't work so now she's going to try an angelfish. She is going to make a treacle tower out of Mexican wedding cake, and there will be plenty of hot – that's spicy hot – savouries. Because she is staying up late planning the party, she doesn't like to get up early in the morning, not that she ever did. She will hold the party Thanksgiving weekend so that Kendra will come, and then they can finally meet Sven. 'I walk out back in the afternoons,' she says, 'and the dogs come with me and try to dig up woodchuck holes. But sometimes I don't want any company.'

Kendra cannot come home. She has to study for an exam,

and besides Sven's family asked her over a long time ago and she already said yes.

The piñata stays hanging in the corner of the dining room where the bird cage used to be before the last finch died. There are no candies inside the piñata – Darlene gets up and shakes it one night when no one's around.

Her science teacher, Mr Duncan, has said ecology will be an everyday word for them by the end of the year. In English, they're reading *To Kill a Mockingbird*. Danny Law, who got his leg caught in a thresher when he was little, has kissed Darlene on a dare. His lips felt like soap suds. She did not touch the knee that won't bend. She was surprised how polite he was about the whole thing. 'If you're ready,' he'd said, 'I'm game.' After that, it didn't embarrass her to sit next to him on the bus. She wouldn't try to sit next to him, but if there weren't any other seats she was happy to sit there. After school, the Grummett sisters call (one from their room, the other using the extension in the basement) to share intelligence with her.

'Feed the dogs,' her mother would say. 'I'm not doing it for you.'

Darlene's diary is full of complaints. *Clean the bathroom, cook supper twice a week, do the dishes every night. Feed the dogs.* She hides her journals on the closet shelf behind the big box of Kotex her mother has bought so that she will not be caught unawares. There is a black elastic belt tucked inside. Darlene does not write in the diary that she hates to go out to the dog pen in the dark, with the wind going through the blue spruce and the stink of the hot kibble mash. Sometimes if the water dish is empty she leaves it that way because it will mean two trips to the chicken coop. The dogs lick and wag, as always.

Darlene's mother goes to Toronto for a week to spend time with Kendra and returns full of examples of the things you can buy in Chinatown: money cards, jade, bamboo steamers, flip flops, back-scratchers, tissue paper cut-outs.

Sven is a lovely young man, tall and blond as the name suggests, and utterly respectful. And he introduced her to the most wonderful sandwich, something called falafel.

Darlene's dad is miffed that he didn't get the requested LP, by America.

Kendra comes for Christmas. The cranberry and popcorn garlands get tossed out the day after she leaves. The windows frame frost.

When Darlene gets home from the first day back at school, the dogs do not come running up to her to say hello.

'Just so you'll know,' her mother says before Darlene has her boots off. 'It was out of kindness. They were so cold out there.'

'They didn't suffer,' Darlene's dad says. 'I can tell you. I took them in. I took the day off school because it was the right thing to do.'

The stairs do not make enough noise under Darlene's feet.

'We didn't give them what they needed,' her dad says outside her door.

'They had steaks this morning,' her mom says. 'In the house.'

Darlene does not speak to her parents for two weeks. When they phone Kendra, she calls them murderers and says she'll never come home again.

Darlene's dad says it's time for her to come off it. He makes her go in to school with him on a Saturday to feed the animals. The boa constrictor is going to shed soon, you can see the dead skin. The gerbils huddle in sawdust. The rats are adorable and the guinea pigs oink the whole time.

Darlene's dad says it wasn't so much his idea about the dogs as it was her mother's. Ever since Kendra left, Linda's been thinking those animals are lonely. Darlene's mother gets oppressed easily, Darlene has to keep that in mind. Ideas are bigger for Linda than they are for other people.

Darlene goes home and takes down the piñata and no one

ever seems to notice. The next day she finds a bottle of amaretto inside the piano bench and sticks it under her father's pillow. She sits on the moss-green bedspread for a while, and puts the bottle back in the bench. There's a photo of Kendra with the dogs in there. Darlene sticks it on the fridge and no one takes it down for years.

❧ St. Jerome ❧

Ivan's house has four walls that don't touch any other walls. Ivan has two legs that don't touch any other legs. The only things he finds in his bed are of no real consequence, except in the event of a fire, where they could save his life if he had enough time to knot the sheets which otherwise are annoying to fold coming out of the dryer and which he never does fold, actually.

'Stop saying about this thing you have for the wind,' his brother Jerome says.

They are in Ivan's kitchen at the back of the house, the room farthest from the Atlantic. Sometimes there's fog out front and sunshine coming in through the kitchen windows.

Jerome talks a lot. 'Say you're trying to open all these like little sardine tins of love you've always known you had inside you.'

'Ask for a can-opener?'

'You don't really want it, do you? You just say you do. Any mention of wind, I quit. The thing is to use the word "open." That's what women want. So they can get right in there.'

'How about I say I'm having an open house tonight and she's the only one invited?'

'I am this close to walking here. Do you ever get that?'

A row house is a chicken coop, but a detached house makes for a lonely rooster.

Row houses chatter. They exhale thumps and door bangs and supper conversations and the sound of water squeezing through shower heads. Most of the houses on his street are joined, one piece of yellow vertical trim denoting that the peeling red house has stopped and the peeling green house has started. A matching plank twelve to seventeen feet away to establish that the green house is now making way for a family that's sweet on pink.

There is always something happening in front of the houses. Right now, two doors down from Ivan's, there's a chaise lounge out on the sidewalk with a woman's oiled body shining up at the sun. Ivan doesn't know her name. She likes to hang laundry out back every good day and uses a pole to prop it up in the middle. Her man is also out on the street, also greasy, lying in the belly-shade of a Ford. This is where he is every day but Ivan can't tell from the feet sticking out whether the man is happy down there.

Going the other way, to the east of Ivan's place, toward downtown and the sliver of St. John's harbour that's visible from his bathroom window, he can see Shirley Locke sitting high up on her steps. Three women sit a couple of steps down from her. They twist their heads up her way and repeat 'You don't say' every once in a while. Shirley starts each sentence with 'What *I* think'. The other women start their sentences with 'What *I* heard'. In twenty minutes or so the women will shake their heads, drop the butts in the peanut butter jar Shirley keeps full of water, brush off the dirt or grass or ants or ash or whatever is attacking their knees and stand up.

Little girls squeak up and down the street. Teen boys keep their hands in their pockets and their shoes slapping. Cats sleep on doormats. Right across the road, a cat sits on the hood of a car. Cats look out windows. Dogs zigzag. Old men spit. Radios advertise.

There is only crumbly sidewalk in front of Ivan's house, no mammals.

Detached houses stand back and sigh.

Ivan knows Shirley Locke because one day as usual the wind sucks his screen door open, only this time her cat runs into his house. She gives a quick knock and goes in after it. She

72

is up in his bedroom by the time he finds her, with the cat in her arms and her cigarette steaming like a little train behind her ear.

'Sorry about the shoes,' she says. 'Forgot.'

Her sandals belly-flop on the stairs. She talks to the cat on the way down. 'I told you. I told you stick close.'

At the door she calls back up to Ivan. 'You need a woman, you know that?'

He looks down at her. The top of her head doesn't look very nice. A lot of scalp showing. 'What's the cat's name?'

'Isis.'

And then she's gone, without even closing the door right.

Ivan goes back into his bedroom. The only thing he can see is that there are a few clothes on the floor and the bed is unmade. He introduces twenty-three pairs of brown, black and sport socks to some Arctic Power. Fourteen briefs. Nineteen T-shirts. One pair of Levis. He has no pants to wear while he's doing the laundry and he forgets to do the jeans first. He pushes the beer bottles that sit on top of the bureau into a square.

Jerome comes over with pizza and beer. The kitchen table and counters are full of newspapers and dishes and books and cartons and flies and beach rocks. So they sit on the bench out back, but Jerome stands after a while because he says the bench feels like it's going to give.

Jerome tells Ivan to hurry up and finish so they can get going on their plan. 'First of all, you have to really want a woman. Because you've had ideas before, right, like with that pigeon coop and also law school. So I need to hear from you now on this one because we can just walk away here.'

'Everyone says I shouldn't be alone.'

'Okay, good, so we're ready to proceed here then? The thing I'm all for about you getting a woman is she'll keep you tip-top, you know? You get a woman, you'll be busy, guaranteed. Okay, so how would you say you see yourself on this one?'

'I could be active.'

'I'm talking are you happy, are you whole? Which I would say you are. I would say you're pretty much okay but kind of shy, kind of different in an unusual way which makes you seem, you know, not the same as anyone else but really you are just like us in the sense of women being crazy and incredible at the same time and you wanting some of that in your life, right? So I'm thinking the perfect woman for you is quiet. So we'll get you a quiet girl, okay?'

'How is Sharon?'

'Squawking for a baby. Non-stop. But am I complaining here? Do you hear me complaining? Take this and buy some stuff. Sharon says cords are nice, you know. She says you'll never look too fancy in cords.'

Jerome calls the next day. Aside from being named Dorcas, she's the real thing. Nice, not fussy. Solid, in every sense. From his office. No one knows why she hasn't been carried off. 'Now you be nice,' he says. 'No goofing off, okay?'

The Mexican restaurant has a view right through the Narrows out into the North Atlantic. The ocean has a small vocabulary: *gale*, *smashed*, *cold*, *missing*, *grey*. It would laugh at words like *siesta* and *fiesta* and then smash them.

Dorcas looks at the menu for a long time. 'What do you want?' she says.

'You sure ask the hard questions.'

'Yeah, I can't decide, either.'

'That's a pretty smock. I mean top. Or should I say blouse?'

Actually, there's a two-inch gap between the two most necessary buttons where he can see the lace bow in the centre of her bra. Ivan hopes she'll tuck her napkin around her neck when the food comes.

She looks down, straightens her back, tugs her shirt down to try to close the vent. 'It's hard having bosoms like this. Always on display.' She looks proud.

'Hands make the best.'

'Pardon?'

'Bras.'

She looks down at her knife. Polishes one side with her napkin without picking it up, then turns it over and does the same thing on the other side. Jerome said to say he was between contracts if the work question came up. Also if there were any weird moments, to keep her talking about herself.

'Do people ever call you "Door" for short?

'Dorrie.'

'Oh. Sorry, Dorrie.'

He laughs at the rhyme but she doesn't. She goes on and on about insensitivity, the name, her childhood, the name, how noble it really is and how she won't let anyone, anyone get in the way of her peace with how she came into this world and so therefore he'll have to look for another pair of boobies to rub his cruddy paws over.

As if. That's the last thing she says. As if it's a complete sentence. She just stops there, grabs her purse and walks out.

Ivan decides to have enchiladas, seeing how Jerome slipped him the money for supper.

The phone rings after he gets home.

'You promised you'd call,' Jerome says.

'I never call.'

'Really? You never call. Yes, you never call. You never call, Ivan, which is an established fact. So I call you. As in right at this moment.'

Ivan says he's not sure a quiet woman is the one for him. Jerome says it'll just take some time, is all.

He calls back the next day at lunch, which wakes Ivan up. Jerome had to force out of Dorcas how the date went. 'I'm just sick here. Sick. Dorcas, that's a class act. I don't have anything here for you right now, buddy. Nothing left in here.'

Night on the street. The moon is as chunky as cabbage. The fog over the south side hills boils across the moon. Wind sends everything on its way.

Boys are making monkey noises. Someone's hammering out back. Someone's yelling inside a house: *I said I would, didn't I?* Ivan takes a chair out of the kitchen and puts it out on the sidewalk, like the row-house people do. No one talks to him. He goes back and gets three beer and sets them by his feet and stays out until two.

Diane has red hair, too, and he almost asks her what colour hair kids with two red-headed parents will have. Diane's not quiet. She's his bank teller. When he wrote 'Lunch?' on a deposit slip so as not to embarrass her in public, she passed back '27th – 12:30 – here'. And she stamped his cheque with real muscle.

When Ivan goes to collect Diane, she's waiting just outside the bank.

'I'd like to take you to a Thai restaurant,' he says.

'I wasn't aware we had one.'

'Well, no, there isn't.'

She looks at him then. But she laughs in a way that makes her eyes even more green against her lime suit. He guides her across the street to the cheap Indian place.

He wonders how the restaurant got the outside of the chicken so red. He studies Diane's smallness, thinking about how she seems to break out of her little frame. She is plump but he's sure if he touched one of her arms it would feel like every ounce of her is essential. He would like to touch both her arms. He would like to hold one of her hands in both of his and rub a thumb over her baby-blue nail polish.

'You must travel if you like Thai food,' she says.

'No, but I've read about it.'

She laughs that laugh again, no hesitating this time.

'What do you do, anyway?'

He tells her he's a consultant. She gives him a twitch of a smile. She lets him pay the bill. He says he'd like to have lunch again and she says, 'When you're back working again, you'll be downtown anyway, right? So let's do it.'

Ivan takes a six-pack out front. He's had two when an eight-year old bums one. 'Don't drink it, though,' Ivan says.

'No way. I'll sell it, sure.'

'How much?'

The boy looks at him. 'For you, fifty cents.'

Someone somewhere out of sight is doing throat ululations like they do in North Africa. It is a pleasant sound and for a moment the whole street is quiet, listening to itself.

Ivan is going to convert his free-standing house into a row house. From now on he's going to pull his chair up on the sidewalk across the street so he can look at his lot in order to draw up the plans.

He's about to tell this to the boy, who is still standing there. But just then a bunch of teens come along and the boy slips in with them, saying, 'Look,' and holding the beer high.

Ivan phones his brother for maybe the twelfth time in his life. He needs fifty bucks. Jerome mentions how he's pretty much covering Ivan's mortgage already. Ivan says it's to get something for Dorcas. Jerome makes Ivan go his office to get the money, and of course he sees her. She turns her head away when he says hi.

At the florist's, he only spends thirty bucks because fifty seems like a lot of money for something that grows in dirt. He writes on the card, 'With Apologies to Dorcas. Sincerely, Ivan the Terrible.' It's formal because he can't say 'Sorry, Dorrie'.

He sends the flowers to her office, so Jerome will see.

Jerome swings over that night after work. He doesn't see Ivan in his chair across the street, so Ivan calls out.

'Well,' Jerome says, 'don't you look right at home.'

Ivan goes and gets another chair.

'Can't we sit in the backyard? I mean, not here, but like your backyard?' Jerome says. TV sounds slurp out the windows behind their heads.

'It's good here.' Ivan makes sure to tell Jerome he asked for permission to sit there because that's the kind of thing Jerome needs to know.

Jerome won't have a beer. He doesn't say much. They watch the dogs. One comes down the street, does some complicated sniffing-and-pissing patterns. As soon as it's gone, another dog goes to all the same places in slightly different order. A couple of houses down, the boys are trying skateboard tricks. Shirley is out on her steps, smoking.

'I like to look at my house,' Ivan says.

'I guess Sharon's waiting for me.'

Jerome and Sharon live in the woods on Indian Meal Line, where there's not so much wind but where the roads are trickier in the winter. That's why they've got the big Jeep. The skateboard guys stand on top of their skateboards to watch it drive off.

Her name is Rose but she is a daisy. She has bought him a pint. She tells him she is an installation artist and that her next project will involve a giant clothesline that will be strung across the Narrows. With giant clothes. Some bloomers, yes, but mostly dresses with polka dots. Turquoise and yellow and orange and purple. Ivan is certain that one day soon he will be able to tell Rose about his house-conversion project.

Which he winds up doing immediately, after she buys him another pint. She loves the idea, she says. She sees something like a false front, making it look like his house is attached on either side. But really only the boards on the face of the house would extend across. Nothing would change but everything would change.

Ivan hadn't considered that. He'd been thinking of removing both sides of his house and making brand new walls.

'You're not really going to do it, are you?'

Ivan nods.

Rose takes someone else's cigarette out of the ashtray. 'Can I say something?'

Ivan nods.

She tells him she's never actually going to do that thing across the harbour, or at least she's pretty sure she's never going to do it. It's just something to get worked up about, something to jazz on about. It's like a way to inhale without choking. All she needs from an idea is juice.

A man taps her on the shoulder. 'Sorry, doll,' she says, and sticks the cigarette right between the man's lips. He pulls out a pack, shakes out a fresh one and lights it for her. She has to flick her hair out of the way. One arm is covered with bangles.

Ivan asks her to dance and she moves in a very beautiful way with her eyes closed and makes him stay up to dance to another song. He believes she has enough bangles that they could toss one or more over each beer bottle on his bureau.

When he gets out of the washroom, she's arm-in-arm with the cigarette man, flicking her hair around. She does look up when Ivan leaves. She comes over and says, 'I know I'll see you again. I always bump into people like you again.'

Jerome's only got ten minutes and he's just stopping for those ten minutes, understood, but there's stuff going on and he's not going to pretend there's not stuff going on because what's the point of not saying it like it is? Which is that maybe Ivan is taking this dating thing too seriously and not everything in life works out. So maybe he should just accept that and stop sitting out on somebody else's sidewalk all the time and maybe he should come and stay with Jerome and Sharon for a few weeks just until he's sorted out again. But only under the proviso that Ivan stays out of Sharon's hair because he knows how hard she tries and how upset and anxious Ivan makes her.

Jerome says all this while he's sitting in his Jeep because there's no way he's going to say it in front of the whole neighbourhood and Ivan doesn't seem to want to walk through his own door of his own house these days, which is funny considering how there was a time when Jerome couldn't ever convince Ivan to leave the place. Jerome and Sharon want to know if Ivan's getting sick again. They want him to come and mellow out at their place. Sharon believes just eating regularly could make for improvements.

Ivan's inside the van, too. The engine's running, which is not cheap these days and which must mean Jerome really is only staying for a short time.

'You just need taking care of, that's the problem,' Jerome says.

'You think I should get a job, right?'

'Are you lonely, Ivan?'

'I kind of got those flowers for you. But not really because you paid for them.'

'I've got four minutes, and Sharon's waiting. You coming?'

Ivan shakes his head. 'Mad?'

'You want to know how it really is? I'm relieved here. I'm breathing again. I mean it for you to come and stay with us but that's not to say I was looking forward to it.'

'But when you first had the idea it made you happy?'

'Yeah.'

'So then everything's good, right?'

'Excepting for this whole thing of what we're going to do with you.'

Rose the daisy is at the post office, behind Ivan in line. Her cheeks are a happy colour against her dyed black hair, which is an unusual thing. She's wearing a skirt with little mirrors all over it.

'Hey there, crazy guy,' she says. 'You should grow that garden you were going on about the other night. I think you should just do it. Start digging, get the old back in crisis, stop thinking about it. Just go.'

'I think you're thinking of someone else.'

'I hate it when people say that. Right now, I'm thinking about you and your garden and it's right here in front of me.' Her hands cover the air between them.

'Will you help me?'

'You don't need help with that, for Christ's sake.'

Ivan points to an open wicket.

'Show me when it's done, OK?'

The clerk's face changes after Rose steps up and plunks her daypack on the floor. She has this way of making everyone awake.

Jerome is in the mood for an after-work beer, so why doesn't Ivan meet him at five? Ivan would have put on the new cords if Sharon was coming, just to settle her.

Ivan gets there pretty late. He pulls out his wallet out to buy a round. Jerome won't let him.

'So?' Ivan says.

'What?'

'You're going to tell me something.'

'Bull. I just want to know what you're going to do now.'

Ivan drinks some beer.

Jerome doesn't touch his. 'Tell me the day I'm not having to look out for you. Tell me when it's coming.'

'We're going to talk about getting a job now, aren't we?'

Jerome doesn't say anything for a couple of minutes. But

then he wants to be candid if that's all right because what's the point of stuffing it down until it rots inside a person? What's the point? Ivan isn't going to get a job. To be clear. Ivan isn't going to get a job and unless he needs money Ivan isn't going to phone his only sibling who is actually by date of birth Ivan's little brother but the thing about real life is nothing plays out normal. Ivan's world is only about Ivan. But the thing is, Jerome's world is mostly about Ivan, too, see? Which would seem unfair on a certain fundamental level, right? But that's how it goes. That's just how it goes.

'I guess I should head out soon,' Ivan says. 'I'm supposed to meet a friend tonight.'

Which he shouldn't have said because it only gets Jerome going more.

What friend is this, Jerome would like to know. Does Ivan actually pick up the phone to speak with this friend? Does this friend spend half the night awake wondering if Ivan's house is going to burn down or if Ivan's got enough food to eat? Does this friend give Ivan his overtime cheque and never say a thing about getting it back?

'My friend doesn't mind me.'

'You don't have a friend. Say it. You don't have any friends. Say "I don't have a friend." You take my money and you lie to me.'

'Want to know something that'll make you happy? I'm not going ahead with converting the house into a row house.'

'Look,' Jerome says. 'I thought a woman would be good. I thought she would lift a load.'

'And nothing's changed.'

'And nothing ever changes.'

'Except the wind.'

'I told you I wouldn't listen to any more of your shit. Your ha-ha-everything's-stupid shit. So just excuse me while I bow out, okay?'

Jerome throws eighty bucks on the table and walks out. Ivan finishes his beer for him. Jerome won't call for a couple of weeks. But he will. He always does.

Shirley comes over when he waves. 'What do you think?' Ivan says. He's moved the bench to the front of the house so that it's sitting on the edge of his sidewalk.

'Wobbles.'

'Beer?'

'It's only early.'

But she doesn't say anything when he comes back from the kitchen with two bottles and a glass for her.

'You wiped that out, did you? Not a clean dish in that house, I'll bet. Hopeless, you are.'

'I used soap. Shirley?'

'Yeah?'

'Don't you think you were named right? You seem very sure about things.'

'Only what's obvious, which is a considerable amount.'

He tells her his brother's nickname is St. Jerome and that his is Ivan the Terrible and that he's thinking to put a big bowl of water out for the animals one of these days.

'Why don't you just do it?' Shirley says.

And so he does. Her cat comes over and scratches its back on the sidewalk.

'Doesn't that feel better?' Shirley says.

'Are you talking to your cat?'

'What I think is that words are for humans.'

She stays for another while, telling him which families to watch out for and which ones are of no consequence. 'You're never alone,' she says.

'No,' he says. 'Never. I've heard that theory, too.'

❧ Visitors ❧

The rustling wakes me. I tell myself it is the cat playing with the bags I've left in the downstairs hallway. Two Glad bags full of clothes for the Sally Ann that have been sitting there since last weekend's closet haul.

Continuous rustling. And the dog's nails tapping around on the hardwood downstairs.

I want the noises to stop. I want the dog to come back up. I am listening so hard my breaths sound volcanic, hot.

Rustling. Clicks. A bump.

I have to stop being so paranoid. I have the phone. I have the phone right here in my room. There is no lock on my door but I have the phone.

But if I call 9-1-1, the police will laugh at me. They'll talk about me: *Yeah, so the boys get to her house and she's all crying and whatnot and it's like, 'Hello, missus, hate to disappoint but the only company around would be ourselves.'* They will double over laughing because this is St. John's, where the cabbies see you in the door before ripping back down the hill. Where you don't worry walking home at 4 a.m. because the nearest house is so close – if anyone was following you, all you'd have to do is lean in and knock. And no one does break-ins on Goodview Street. Thieves don't steal from neighbours. Thieves go to Cowan Heights, Waterford Bridge Road, places where there's a lot more worth taking.

The rumble of the patio doors. Or what sounds like them. I've been mistaken about that before. That other time, it was only a man trying to open the side gate. Drunk, probably. Got his short cuts mixed up, maybe. But he was there, although I didn't see him when I ran downstairs to turn the light on over the back deck. It was all I could think to do, get downstairs and get that light on. Nothing. I knew I should look in the cellar to be sure, except I couldn't go down in case he was there. I decided to go out on the street and check the basement windows from the outside. They were shiny and whole. I think I laughed at myself then, out on the street at five-thirty in the morning in a nightie, bare feet in big white Sorrels. And then I saw the gate that leads into the backyard. Open.

The police officer looked around with his flashlight and then came in to talk to me, kicking the snow off his boots. He said there'd been a caller, all right, someone with big feet by the look of his prints. They showed he hadn't come all the way up to the back door. Probably scared off by the lights flicking on, the officer said. A nice man, tired. I wanted him to check the basement but couldn't bring myself to trouble him.

And now it's happening again.

I have to get up. I have to get up even though I want to stay in this one position, curled tight on the bed with my good ear up. If I am still enough and listen hard enough, I will turn into butter and melt into the sheets. And when my house is quiet again, I will settle back into my regular self. But I can't just stay curled up here. I must at least stand, show I am solid. I get up and walk to the hallway, phone in hand, and look over the banister.

Silence.

He has tried and given up.

I decide to go into the next room, unhook my cement-block of a computer and push it up against my bedroom door, for security. I jiggle cords. A scurry from down there. I run back to the landing, my feet crashing on the pine boards.

I listen. Nothing.

I can't go downstairs because someone is there.

I can't call 9-1-1 because no one's there.

The bathroom door has a lock and a window that I can yell out of if I need to. I take my comforter and pillow and the phone into the bathroom. The dog comes up. I bolt the door and we settle on the tiles. I feel very safe. I'm ready to rib myself come morning. I sleep well.

Martin is angry. Why didn't I call the police? Why didn't I call him? I can't explain. I say I understood the intruder was there but wouldn't let myself know it. Martin says he's too mad to talk.

My visitor wedged a stick in the door to the basement to prop it open and keep the noise down. I pull it out and the hinges talk. Down there, he saw nothing worth taking. Piles of kindling for the wood stove, a push mower. A washer and dryer. Clutter. He found the main floor more attractive. I'm looking everywhere for my watch when the phone rings again. It's Martin again, to clarify. He's frustrated, not angry, and he doesn't understand me. He's worried about me. So are Carl and Pontiac, and they've been talking and they all want to come over and cook me supper, pamper me.

'But I can't even buy a bottle of wine,' I say. 'He got my wallet.'

'We're bringing everything,' Martin says.

'You mean Ooma and Louise are bringing supper?'

'No,' he says. 'It's just us guys coming.'

'Why?'

'It's important.'

When Martin arrives, I've just finished throwing out the newspapers the police officer used for fingerprinting. One jar of powder looked like ground charcoal, the other like baking soda. He'd mixed both together on the papers, but only the dark one shows now. It gets on my fingers and shines like black pearls and doesn't want to be washed off. It's still on my hands as Martin gives me a hug. We kiss.

'I'm okay,' I say.

'I'm not.'

He has a canvas bag to empty – portobello mushrooms, asparagus, two bottles of red wine. A big cast-iron frying pan.

I point to the window above the sink. There's a criss-cross on it, black powder. Martin goes over and tries to open it.

I say, 'You can't, the guy's ass bent the arm.'

The window opens out. I crank it closed at night. Except last night I forgot. He was skinny, my thief. He'd balanced on the palings of the picket fence and cut the screen with a knife. Then he'd squeezed in. My neighbour, Johnny, had to stand on the fence to force the window shut again. Managed to get it locked, which he said is the main thing until I get it fixed.

'This makes me crazy,' Martin says.

'It was a B&E and I left the window open. That's all.'

'We had to come tonight,' Martin says. He stares out the window.

I take his elbow. 'Let me show you what good taste my visitor had.'

The thief's intentions are still laid out on the couch. My sleeping bag. A ghetto blaster. A Polaroid camera. My CDs. All in plastic shopping bags. My panic stomp had interrupted him, possibly scared him.

Constable Turpin said the man who was in my house would have been thinking in blocks of five. Five bucks for the sleeping bag, five bucks for two CDs, ten for the cassette player.

'Why didn't you call?' Martin says again. But he softens a bit, tells me to go upstairs and soak in the bath.

I am in the tub when Pontiac and Carl arrive. I hear them walking around inside, Martin leading. They open the squeaky door to the hall closet, where my satchel used to hang on a nail. I hear the sliding doors open, their feet on the deck. Then they come back down the main hallway. Shoes kick off but the stairs to the second floor still complain under their weight.

'Hey, sweetie.' Carl's voice.

'Hi,' I say.

'It's me and Carl,' Pontiac says.

'Yeah,' I say, 'I know.'

Pontiac: 'What're you at?'

I splash some water.

Carl: 'You take your time.'

Pontiac: 'And sing out if you need a back scrub.'

'There's a lock on that door, buddy.'

Their feet boom down the steps. I am happy tired from the glass of wine Martin made me take upstairs. My blood scrubs the leftover adrenaline away. I fall asleep, until the water cools off enough to wake me.

They're talking downstairs, a low vibration as they shuffle silverware and rattle the pots.

'You smell some good,' Pontiac says. Martin and Carl both nod.

I say, 'Let me do something.'

'No way,' Carl says. 'You sit right here.' He pulls out a chair from the breakfast table. 'Tomorrow we're putting motion detector lights out back.'

'Thanks, but I'm okay.'

Martin is heading to the deck with a plate of steaks Carl and Pontiac must have brought. The dog is right behind. Martin stops, looks at her. 'Where was it last night?'

I snort. 'Apparently showing the nice man where I keep my purse until she got bored and came back up.'

Martin: 'Stupid animal.'

Me: 'Hey.'

Pontiac: 'See that wind last night?'

Martin: 'Well, she is.' He goes outside.

Pontiac: 'It's innocence, is all.'

Carl is tearing lettuce. He looks at Pontiac, who is leaning against the counter and tells him to get going with the garlic bread.

Me: 'How's Louise?'

Carl: 'Good, excellent.'

Me: 'I wanted her to come tonight. And Ooma.'

Pontiac: 'Yeah, she was real curious about what we're doing tonight.'

Me: 'So why didn't you bring her?'

Carl: 'It's not a celebration.'

Pontiac: 'Yeah, like we're feeling kind of slam-dunked here.'

'Oh,' I say. I tell them I'm feeling a little bit lucky.

Raindrops measle the deck. Martin leans on the rail, looking into the backyard. I put my hand on the small of his back.

'Why didn't you call?' He's looking straight ahead, talking quietly.

'Shouldn't cook when you're mad,' I say.

He turns to face me. 'It's disappointment.'

The rain is making the fat on the barbecue antsy. It ticks and jumps. One of the steaks is on fire. He picks it up with a fork and the flame disappears. He sets the meat back on the grill and stands there, waiting. 'I'm trying to be in this thing. You going to let me in?'

'It's flaming again,' I say.

Carl is a careful man and makes his salad dressing just so. It is creamy from egg yolk and mustard, and tastes warm on the tongue, not sharp. Pontiac has overcooked the asparagus. He apologizes, but I tell him it's hard to time with the steaks. Someone – probably Pontiac – has lit candles on the table. He says there should be flowers, too. I remind him it's not supposed to be a party as I fill glasses with their wine.

'We're just trying to make it up to you,' he says. 'What I can't get is why you didn't call the police straight away.'

Martin is watching me. Carl, too, but not in the same way.

I say, 'Why do I have to defend my actions in my own house?'

Martin: 'Why are you so defensive?'

'Can't we talk about movies or something?' No one answers me. 'It's like everyone is saying I had all these choices.'

Carl: 'No, doll. That's not it. We just want to understand.'

'I don't know.' My voice tightens and I can't get it loose. 'If I got on the phone, he'd know there was a woman upstairs. Alone.' I drink some wine, try to push it down.

Carl: 'But sweetie, he already knew it was a woman when he heard you moving around up there. A man would have run at him.'

Pontiac: 'Yeah, guys have these territorial lines, right? And if you're in my house you're crossing them big-time, bud, and I'm coming at you, so MOVE.'

'Whereas women don't do that. We're inclined to share.'

'Whoa,' Pontiac says. 'Whoa.'

Carl: 'Just to establish something here, we fucking hate this guy, too.'

Martin: 'But next time you have to phone someone right away. I mean, if it ever happens again. You call me, okay?'

I attempt to smile. 'Why are you guys here, anyway?'

Martin tells the other two to go out and bring back some beer. He sits on the couch and pats the middle cushion next to him. I see someone's cleared the sofa while I was in the tub – probably Martin. My CDs are back on the shelf. The sleeping bag is on the floor.

'Come here,' he says. I shake my head. He gets up and takes my hand and I let him pull me from the table.

'Knock, knock,' Pontiac says through the mail slot when they come back. He gives me a one-armed hug in the hallway, and I can feel his hair swinging against my breasts. A twelve-pack is pulling down his right arm. Carl gives me a little punch on the shoulder and carries a lemon meringue pie into the kitchen. 'I think we should clear out pretty soon,' he says. 'You look beat out.'

'I just want to do this one thing first,' Martin says, coming in from the living room.

'Oh yeah,' says Pontiac, 'we were going to do that, weren't we?'

'Stand here,' Martin says, pulling me so that I'm right under the light. 'We're going to spot you. Just let yourself fall and whichever way you do, we'll catch you.'

'This is cracked,' I say. 'Is this what you do at all those supposed meetings?'

'Mostly we talk,' Carl says. 'We're really trying to talk.'

'Come on,' Martin says. 'Let's go.'

'Do I have to?' I say, but I imagine tilting into a hammock, into a lazy wraparound net. I want to try. I look at Martin and fall toward him. I catch myself. I try again. My toes catch. I can't do it. He tells me to close my eyes. I let myself tip back. I can hear them shifting their weight, getting ready. But I catch myself again. 'I want to,' I say.

'Take your time.' Carl's voice.

I keep my eyes closed as I turn around a couple of times so I won't know who is where. I try falling to my left. I can't.

'Come on,' says Martin, 'you can do it.' Like he says in bed, earnest, urgent. I wobble. 'Now,' he says. I turn again so I won't know where he is. I can do this. I'm going to do this. I'm falling forward, I'm being pulled by taffy. It's going to happen. But as my heels lift, Carl says, 'Okay, okay, there you go.'

I put a foot forward to stop. 'I think I need quiet.' I cross my arms.

Pontiac asks if he can try.

I step out of the centre and he slides in. Pontiac closes his eyes and smiles. He bullets down like an old man fainting, straight out. Martin catches him. Carl and I are right behind, ready.

'Sweet,' Pontiac yells. 'Oh God, sweet.'

Pontiac catches Martin, and then Carl tries. He'll freeze, too, I think. But he comes straight for me and staggers me with his weight, an astronaut's grin on his face. I right him in my arms.

'Give it another go, girl,' Pontiac says.

I step back into the centre but I'm trying too hard.

'We don't bite,' Carl says.

I excuse myself and pop up to the bathroom for a while.

'Okay,' says Pontiac, 'how come you said before you felt lucky?'

He's sitting on the woodbox. Carl's in the big chair. Martin and I are back on the couch. We all pick pie crumbs off our plates with licked fingers. We've decided pie is perfect with beer.

'Let's give her a break, shall we?' Carl says. 'You can see the woman's about to drop.'

'No,' I say, 'it's okay.'

'We're here,' says Martin.

'This man walks into my house and doesn't touch me. I mean, he's not even thinking of it. It's a money thing, not a sex thing. So it was good.'

Martin: 'But you said before that you're angry.'

Pontiac: 'Yeah, he still messed with your power.'

Me: 'It was for money. So I'm seeing that all this fear I've had is pretty screwed up.'

Carl: 'Men are shits.' We stop and look at him. 'Well, we are, we do crappy things.'

Pontiac: 'Yeah, like rape and war and that shit.'

Carl: 'No, I'm pinpointing how we just fuck off whenever we want.'

Pontiac: 'Like on what level are you talking?'

Carl: 'Like leaving Louise.'

Martin: 'Fuck, why didn't you say something?'

Carl: 'No, I'm not leaving her. I'm just saying I could, you know.'

Me: 'She could check out of the hotel, too, you know.'

Carl: 'But that's the thing. She won't.'

Pontiac laughs his hee-haw donkey laugh. 'Get wise, my friend.' They let me take their plates into the kitchen. Pontiac keeps interrupting Carl and saying, 'No, you don't get it, my friend.'

The moon is coming through the intruder's window. The kitchen is hot and I can't open the window. I pull open the sliding glass door in the dining room and step onto the deck. The wind makes me shiver. I go back in.

'Guys,' I say, 'I love you but you have to clear out.'

'Feel any better, sweets?' Carl asks.

I say yes.

Carl zips up, promising he won't drive, that he'll get his car in the morning. Pontiac's going to walk with him. He buttons his long black coat.

'Thanks, guys,' I say. 'Really, I appreciate it.' We hug quickly and they thump down the porch stairs. Martin wants to stay, but I shake my head.

'Come on,' he says, 'I'm worried.'

I say no.

'You'll sleep better.'

I say no.

'Come on,' he says again.

I stand there.

'Okay,' he says, 'you can take care of yourself.'

Yeah, I say.

I fall into a thick sleep, a chair under the doorknob. I wake to hear the dog's nails snicking around on the floor and a pounding sound. It's two-thirty. The pounding keeps going. I release the chair, flap down the stairs in my robe. I'm not afraid. Two nights in a row, what are the chances?

'Misty,' a man is saying. 'Misty, open up.'

He's got the screen door open. I can see his head through the window in the wooden door. He's maybe fifty-five. I talk through the door. 'Go home out of it.'

He pushes the mail slot open, bends to look in. 'Misty,' he says, 'let me in, love.'

I try to push the flap back down but even through the flap I can feel he has thick fingers. 'There is no Misty here. Wrong house, skipper.'

'Oh,' he says. 'Whoopsy doodle.' He makes sure the screen door is closed so the wind won't catch it and then takes small drunk steps down the hill.

I try to sleep again. I put the chair back. It makes me feel good in the same way full cupboards do. But then I hear a noise in the back yard. Rustling. I get out of bed and squat down by the window, staring between the slats of the blind. I can see my neighbour's shed and the fence my burglar balanced on last night. The wind is up. It's probably just twigs scraping on the trees. My eyes dart around. If Martin was here, I'd be sound asleep or whispering in his ear.

.

❧ Giulione's Zipper ❧

Giulione and those shoes. Steel-tipped, actually click-clicking when the man walks. Like he has to let everyone know he's around. Jill is quite sure she hates Giulione. Everything goes well for him. He does not get creamy salad-dressing stains on his pants just before wooing a client. In the middle of a seductive pitch, he does not forget what he is saying. His car works when required, as required, and therefore is not waiting to be towed to the auto wreckers. Which means Giulione would not have taken the wrong bus to City Hall today and not had to run the last six blocks in the rain. His smile would have been as crisp as the manila envelope he'd passed over at the counter at city planning, probably at a cool 3:20 in the afternoon, well before Jill's 4:57 deadline panic.

Another reason to hate Giulione: it's his fault everything is messed up.

Breathe, breathe. Light in, shadows out. No, not shadows exactly: anxiety brought on by Jill's emerging vulnerability. Her counsellor is trying to get her to look at things in a more healthy, less desperate light. To catch her thoughts and send the unhelpful ones packing.

It's clear to Jill that she's been pushing down her needs lately and that they've been pushing right back. She ignored them and now she's paying the price. But she's had no time to try to fit them in, not with the bid on the skateboard bowl and the horrible sense that, hard as the work is, it isn't hard enough. Late at night, going over the plans, she can only imagine that no matter what she settles on, Giulione's design will be better. Jill has paid particular attention to what she calls the 'greening of the pit', believing that the blue-haired matrons on the committee will love a design that hides what it really is – a concrete

97

bowl full of cocky teen-aged boys. Her plan includes two ingenious tunnels – strictly one-way, of course, and bright and wide inside. She believes the effect will be spectacular – there will be a brief but heady thrill for the show-off rider in being alone for that second or two inside the tunnel waiting to pop up and out, possibly doing a three-sixty before turning and sliding down the next tunnel, only to reappear at the opposite end. A thatch of wild flowers will cover the shallow dome over the tunnel. There will be a certain expense involved, yes, but the blue-hairs will love it. And Jill is ready for adventure. This is whimsy on a grand scale. It felt so good, so loose, drawing up the initial plans. And she's consulted a couple of engineers who tell her the structural supports will be a cinch. She feels in her gut her design should win.

But she worries. There is always Giulione. His estimate will probably come in under hers – he's pulled that trick many times before. Maybe he'll take a conventional approach, but probably not. Knowing Giulione, he just might incorporate something like an elegant pool in the centre of the bowl that could double as a water hazard for the skateboarders. He's killer, that one. Everyone loves his work to pieces.

Although he's not above conniving to get what he wants. Only a couple of months ago, he'd invited Jill to his office. It was late on a Friday afternoon and he offered her some Scotch and she accepted just to prove she wasn't a prude. Even though she knew what it was really all about – him trying to get her to spill her guts on the bid for the skateboard park. For her part, Jill hoped to catch even the tiniest glimpse of his design. And to crow a little – just the Saturday before there'd been a big feature in the *Gleaner* on the playground she'd drawn up for the Lions Club.

There was nothing about Giulione that didn't make her jealous. He even had a little refrigerator in his office. Right behind his desk, so that to get ice cubes for their drinks he'd only had to swivel a bit.

Jill had carefully sipped the Scotch Giulione handed her. The fact that it tasted like wormy bog helped. But no matter how she nursed the drink, it still made her feel invincible. Scotch always did that to her. Usually, it just meant she was in danger of walking in front of moving cars. But that Friday, on the eighteenth of March, she'd done something even more ridiculous – she'd held Giulione's penis in her hands.

She can see now that it was a desire to take control. She can see it was her showing a little creativity, even. Her body reminding her it needed more down time. But when it happened, there weren't many thoughts associated with the grab. It had felt like the only thing to do. There'd been a brief feeling of elation at feeling him get hard, but horror struck in the elevator on the way out. She'd walked over to a man and unzipped him in broad daylight. Even worse, it was Giulione. Giulione, whose smirk got even wider. Saying he was flattered but hurrying her out of his pants all the same.

Well, if he didn't like capable hands surprising him, he shouldn't have messed her up with that Oban Scotch, should he?

And he really did fuck her up. She had to go home to her sweet teddy bear Darcy that night even though she was still quaking in her leopard-skin trouser socks. Jill was forced to act as if she was still pure and as if Darcy were still as interesting to her, as if she didn't feel the slightest bit terrible about the urges Giulione had brought out in her.

Jill suffered immensely. And it didn't help that Darcy was a good man, a steady man. He was like a gradual hill – always there, but hardly noticeable. His constancy made her feel even more alone after the penis incident: she just didn't feel bad enough about the terrible betrayal of Darcy's trust, even when he took her to a crazily expensive restaurant the next day. It was their seventh anniversary. He gave her freshwater pearls and matching earrings and kissed her neck in irresistible ways on the cab ride home. All night, she pretended it was Giulione being such a doll. Until Darcy begged her not to put her diaphragm in and she had to chide him a little for being tipsy.

The next Monday, she heaved open the Yellow Pages and signed herself up for a ten-session package with a counsellor named Inez. 'There's this trick with Spanish I tell all my clients about,' Inez said at their first meeting. 'If you drop something, you say, *me cayó*. Which does not translate as *I dropped it*, but rather *it fell from me*.' Jill liked Inez from the start. It's not what you do but how you react that makes you. Jill could steer her boat by the constellation of guilt and always return to the same port. Or she could discover a compassionate ocean and ride and ride.

Jill has gone to nine sessions already. She dreads attending the tenth and final one, but Inez has already told Jill she is ready to stand on her own. Inez is dead set against the idea of clients setting up a semi-permanent relationship with her. She will be available in the event of future emergencies. But Inez says seeing her every week would be as strange as speaking with a priest every week. 'You wouldn't do that, would you?' Inez had asked. 'I mean if you were religious? Even if you had a baby that just died or something?' And Jill had to agree.

She likes that Inez doesn't want her clients in a state of constant crisis. Inez is a soother, not a disturber. She has made Jill feel oodles better. For instance, Inez has helped Jill see her moment of regret is not written in India ink. A penis can always be tucked back inside a fly. And so Jill has worked to modify the experience, to use it to her advantage. She's started making love to Darcy the way a barrel rolls over a cliff – with unstoppable force. Not that he's been completely compliant. The first time Jill re-enacted unzipping Giulione (as an expression of both closure and loyalty), Darcy had said, 'Hey,' in a less than ear-nuzzling way, although he did push his hands over her breasts as he extracted the newspaper that had become crushed between their chests. And after, he did commend what he called her commando attack even though he claimed to have been frightened at first. There was something fierce about her, something funny.

Of course, Jill has not told Darcy about Giulione's zipper. She's never once mentioned his name. Darcy would cry and Jill would tire of trying to comfort him. Plus Darcy would want to revert back to kinder, more quiet sex.

But today, everything has changed. It's been a day of deadlines. First the skateboard park proposal, and now clearly her time with Darcy is up.

She hadn't meant to be so brazen on the bus home from City Hall. It just happened, and if Darcy doesn't believe that when she tells him, well, what can she do? It was mostly innocent anyway. A bit of shoulder-locking with the man sitting beside her. Jill had leaned into the man a littler harder than necessary, that's all. Her left elbow could feel each one of his breaths through his right elbow. Her hand on that side had started rubbing the outside of his thigh a little. Very nonchalantly, very lightly, almost as if she were scratching her own slightly itchy leg. She couldn't stop thinking about the man's bald head and how she wanted it rolling over her, how she wanted to feel its shininess lolling under her arms, under her breasts, against the thickest part of her thighs.

Possibly, she'd rubbed too hard. Or maybe the intensity of the shoulder-squeezing linked-breathing had scared him off. Surely he'd not been oblivious to the whole thing; after all, he did get up and move forward to an empty seat a couple of rows up. Maybe he was thinking of his wife, if he had one, and how he respected her too much to continue being intimate with this exquisite stranger on the bus. He pulled the bell cord and got off without looking back. Jill had to admire him even as she missed him enormously.

When she tried to remember exactly what he looked like, she saw Giulione's face. Which meant, of course, that her life with Darcy was a sham. She understood this even before she reached her bus stop.

Inez would ask what linked the men. The imaginary Inez sounded much more shrill in Jill's head than the real Inez. The real Inez was kind and accepting and would be a marigold if she were a flower.

The only commonality Jill could find between Giulione and Baldy was the fact that both wore goatees.

Inez would ask what that suggested to her.

Jill would answer, 'Being pointy and evil and delicious.'

'And how would Darcy look in a goatee?'

'Like my teddy bear man with fuzz on his chin.'

'Sexy?'

There would be a snort from Jill.

'You believe Giulione is powerful. What about this guy on the bus?'

And that's where Jill is stumped. Giulione and Baldy are not at all alike. They are also not one bit like Darcy. She makes a mental note to think about it some more later on tonight: her final session with Inez is set for tomorrow.

Darcy meets her at the door and she kisses him meaningfully. But she is still going to have to leave him. For his own protection during what is clearly her late-blooming sexual exploration phase. Jill thinks about the right words all through supper. What she settles on, what she decides to say is: 'Maybe we should chill out for a while.' An odd choice of words – she is not normally given to slang. But then again, she isn't used to thinking about the end of a relationship.

She wants to sound casual and slightly hopeful to ease the sting. But what comes out is a burp. Darcy doesn't seem to notice, although it certainly throws Jill. In fact, his lack of awareness makes her feel annoyed with him. He knows she can't digest onions, especially raw onions, and yet what is floating around in the tomato salad he's made? Onion chunks, and not even the sweet purple kind but regular under-the-counter yellow ones.

What is it about men and their primitive taste buds? Burnt toast, horseradish, Stilton cheese, rounds of onion: Jill could slap together that exact sandwich, and Darcy would happily wash it down with something like Oban Scotch before marching her into the bedroom and trying to reward her.

Oh, oh, catty again. No, wrong word. Jill tries to think of a better one. Inez told Jill to start writing her own little thesaurus, to replace words of self-judgement with less brittle, more complex words. Jill is feeling … Jill is feeling silly in a certain detached way. Witty. Sharp-eyed, a truth-explorer.

With supper over, there is no better time to release Darcy from their false bond. They are both still at the table and Jill has recovered from the indignity of the burp. Still, the only decent thing to do is to go swish some mouthwash around first and kill the onion breath.

In the bathroom, she decides to floss and check for black-heads. And then somehow she is in the tub, trapping milky bubbles between her palms and listening to her heart boom bass in the heat. Jill plays the pop-up game with her breasts, sucking her upper back down and into a deep C until not even her nipples show, and then letting them explode up past the skin of water. She let her ears slip under and imagines the phone is ringing but that she can't hear it. This makes her feel so laughy that she does it several times, wishing there were a mirror on the ceiling so she could study what she looks like in this lighter state. She closes her eyes instead. This is nurturing. This is the troubleshooting Inez keeps talking about. It is so easy it almost frightens her. If only Jill had relaxed like this more often, perhaps she wouldn't have been so quick to push the bald stranger's head (and the lips attached to said head) so close to her fuse box. Imaginary lips, of course, but she'd felt them there on the bus. In fact, she'd dared them to give her a jolt. It felt very real. And who, in such a situation, would not welcome the intrusion of reality? Who would cross their legs?

Not Jill. This is beautifully clear to her now. She needs to be free. She wants more than to just open her legs whenever she feels like it – although that would be a start. She wants to float around on her back like a sea otter. Just fool around and go wherever she wants whenever she wants. Cracking mussels on her chest the odd time she gets hungry.

'Oh,' she says because Darcy is right there, standing over her in the bathtub when she opens her eyes. She owes him so much – she does know that – but she needs him to go away. She stays submerged with closed eyes for what feels like ten minutes. The water is getting cold and starting to irritate her skin but she doesn't move in case he is there. When she peeks, he's gone. So are all the bubbles.

Jill stands in front of the mirror for several minutes, trying to think of a secret message to write on it. She thinks about *¡Caramba!* (an expression Inez recommended as a delightful Spanish way to express frustration).

In the end, she writes 'Jill'.

She decides that if Giulione wins the contract bid, she'll allow herself to sink into a full-scale depression. But no point expecting the worst – the announcement won't come for at least a couple of months. She will go out tomorrow and pick up a lovely dress. To think ahead, to get ready for success.

But she won't go shopping. Suddenly, she can see her design is ridiculous and why does she only understand it now that the bid is locked away and there is no way she can snatch it back? A covered, tunnelled skateboard bowl? What was she thinking? Why didn't she do even three minutes of research?

Of course Giulione will win the contract.

Maybe, she thinks, all I really want is a pair of shoes that click when I walk.

Jill wipes her name off the mirror. She tries to look at herself through the hole in the fog but it fills in instantly with more fog.

She is ready. She goes into the bedroom where Darcy is reading *Canadian Geographic*. She's thought of a new way to break it to him, to say something more true to her nature. She is going to say, 'I think there could be some exciting opportunities for each of us.' As a starter, as indisputable non-blaming confirmation of their differences. She is going to be so gentle and kind.

Darcy's magazine has a picture of a lynx on the cover. He is still reading when she opens her mouth, walking toward the bed wrapped in one of her giant towels, her clothes scrunched up in her arm.

What comes out is, 'I'm a bad person.'

Darcy tosses the magazine aside as if it were a grenade and scoops his arms around her. 'What's wrong, pumpkin?' he keeps saying. But Jill can't think of another thing to say. She wants to hit him for making everything worse.

❧ The Simple Truth ❧

Ellen could make stuff up if she wanted to – plenty do up here in Labrador, all it takes is one night on the beer at Trapper's Cabin to figure that out. People let slip that although they've always made out to the contrary, they're still a couple courses – actually six – short of a degree. Or how, despite all the talk about being as free as caribou, they're actually sending cheques to three kids down south.

Ellen is candid when it comes to telling people about her father. There's the time the Mixmaster fell off its pegboard hook because her brother Cole's head was hitting the wall. And how after, whenever she made peanut butter cookies and her family-famous johnnycake, her thumb would rub the hard yellow drips where her mother had glued the handle back together.

There's the story about how her still-married dad took up with the already-married neighbour and how they moved in together for a while until the neighbour cracked up and went away for a rest. And maybe Ellen would go on to tell about life after the divorce, perhaps about the year her mom cooked cow's heart for Christmas because that was all the money there was. Or how Ellen put nine blankets on her bed that winter because her mom kept the furnace down so low.

From there, Ellen might move on to how her mother had to lock up her pottery studio and work around-the-clock shifts in a factory that produced weather-stripping for cars, and how one night during that time her mom came home just past midnight and shouted at Ellen and her older brother, Cole, to get out of bed and come downstairs because they hadn't done the dishes like she'd told them to.

These things all happened, and Ellen knows they've marked

her, have left an aura that sometimes even she can see.

There are decent memories, including some of her father – that time he marched with the farmers, how he went out of his way to give people the finest and most genuine compliments she'd ever heard, that time he bought her a boxed set of *Anne of Green Gables* books for no special reason, even though it cost fifteen dollars. Ellen makes a point of including these details.

But there is one thing she does not talk about. It goes back to when she moved from Quebec to California when she was twelve. What she tells people is that her mother's second marriage was to an American. Technically, this is true, although Andy became American long after they reached the States.

Really, it was her dad who started things. Because after he moved out, Ellen's mom decided it was time to learn some self-defence. And so she signed up for judo classes at the Y. But when she came home with a sprained ankle after the second session, she decided to move on to something gentler. That turned out to be yoga, and Andy was the teacher. He was soft-spoken and smiled a lot. He had long hair and a beard and a lot of people said he looked like J. C. Andy didn't have asthma like her dad, which meant Ellen could have a cat in the house. Her brother, Cole, followed Andy around like a duckling, except he was taller than Andy. The two of them spent a lot of time working on their yogic breathing; Andy said Cole was a natural. Best of all, Andy made their mom laugh, except for the time he held her upside down just for fun and dropped her on her head by accident and she blanked out for a minute. Otherwise, Andy didn't hurt people. Andy didn't shout in the morning or at lunch or in the middle of the night. Andy loved answering questions and never told Ellen or Cole to buzz off.

The not-so-good thing about Andy was he got Ellen's mom meditating and reading books by people with names like Ram Das and Baba Hari Das. And that was bad because more than anything Andy wanted to go live and pray with the man whose books he liked best of all: Swami Sananda, who had set up a 'spiritual community' called Peace Hills in northern California. Cole thought it was an awesome idea. And Ellen's mom was making noises like she'd like to live there, too.

This is what Ellen said during the first phone call she ever made to her father: 'I can make spaghetti. And also I know how to make borscht and tollhouse cookies.' She didn't really want to live with him; she was afraid of him even though he'd stopped being so mad all the time. But he was still unpredictable. Sometimes burnt toast made him laugh and sometimes it didn't. Except anything would be better than California.

He told her he already knew about Peace Hills because her mom had written. He thought it was a crime that her mother wanted to take her to that cult. He absolutely understood that Ellen was in a hard spot and that he was worried like a nutcase about her, but that he'd have to think for a while before deciding something so important.

A couple of weeks later his letter arrived in the mail. *I have been too much of a mess-up to learn now.* It was a hell of a letter for him to write, he said, so much so that he felt like each word was being scritched into his skin. But Ellen had to recognize he was braving the truth, which was that he was not fit to be an everyday dad. So she couldn't come live with him. But he hurt for her and thought she should go into foster care because her mother was also clearly unfit. He would help her make the arrangements if she chose to try out a whole other family. He felt it would be just a lot better for her to start over again with a new family.

Ellen showed the letter to Cole, who called their dad right away and said what a perfect time to work on opening up his heart chakra. Everything is forgiven in time, Cole said. And not to worry because Ellen was a lot better off going to California, and being with her real family, her only family.

Ellen's mother said they should see their father face-to-face this one last time before they headed off to the States. Cole wouldn't go. He was eighteen, and besides, anyone old enough to spell autonomy had certain rights.

Ellen's father had saved extra pop bottles for her to cash in. And when he heated up some vegetable soup for her lunch, he brought it out with curly corn chips on top.

He got her to the train station three-quarters of an hour early like he always did. He looked down at the tiles on the station floor a lot or looked away and gave her a little wink any time their faces met. The tiles were muddy from the thaw. Ellen thought she saw a silhouette of a rabbit in one of the boot-tracks. When the train came, her dad didn't say anything. He waited on the platform until the train started hissing east toward Quebec. Ellen could see him from her window, pacing, or just looking straight at her, crying. She started, too, even though there was a lady sitting next to her, and Ellen was afraid the woman would ask what the trouble was. Ellen couldn't stop until a long time after her father had been replaced by willow trees and fields that still had furrows of snow in them.

She cried almost all the way to the American border. She would have kept on crying as they crossed into the States, except Andy pulled over and her mom passed back Kleenex and a comb and told Ellen to stop it. Cole stayed out of it, for a change.

Her mom and Andy were flat-out nice as they showed the customs officer their birth certificates, her mom unfolding a big square of yellowed paper and laughing about how that's what you got for being born in New Brunswick a long time ago. Ellen's mom remarked on how you couldn't beat the apple blossoms here in the Eastern Townships. And how much they were looking forward to camping in Vermont, even if it was just for the weekend.

Which – considering there was a sewing machine and

Christmas cookbooks but no tent under the tarp in the back of their old Volvo – explained the threat in her voice when she'd told Ellen to stop crying.

The border man waved them through without lifting the tarp. The crossing was near St. Benoit du Lac, a monastery that her mom and Andy would go to sometimes on Sundays to hear Gregorian chanting. One time they'd made Ellen go, too. She'd pressed her fingernails into her legs the whole time, afraid the men in ivory robes would make her do something, like swing the incense holders or carry the silver box full of bones.

A few miles across the border, Andy pulled into a gas station. As soon as the car stopped, he and Ellen's mom held hands for a couple of minutes. Then he started the engine again. He never did get gas, just went straight back to the highway.

During the trip, Ellen's mom bought them lemon yogurt and didn't say anything about the sugar. She cross-stitched her wedding dress. She read Stephen Leacock and Lewis Carroll out loud because Andy hadn't grown up in a reading house. She was anxious to get him started on *Huckleberry Finn*.

Andy went on about all the places they were seeing, and how he'd already hitch-hiked through most of them at some point. The exception being Salt Lake City, which wasn't a thumber's kind of town. He was hoping they could stop off for a couple of days and check out the Tabernacle Choir. Cole said he didn't think that was necessarily a great idea. Sometimes he sat in the full lotus in the back seat with his knee extending into Ellen's half but she didn't complain because she knew her mom would tell her to focus on the idea of cooperation, since it was going to be such a big part in all of their lives now.

Ellen kept her watch on Quebec time. She slept a lot. She didn't pay attention until they were almost there. She liked the strangeness of Wyoming, with its small black mountains and the clouds pushing right down into the flats of brown grass.

And not so long after that they were on a very long back highway in northern California, Andy driving slow, all of them craning to find the right turn-off. There were pick-up trucks and bikers with Mennonite-style beards on the highway. No other Volvos. There were trailer homes with busted-up cars in their driveways. 'Gold everywhere,' Andy said. 'Those would be the Sierra Nevada foothills.'

Ellen's mom saw the cut-off first and pointed at it without saying anything. Down a washboard road for a little way, dust startling up behind them. Then some buildings ahead – what looked to be a small post office and what was for sure a general store. Andy stopped the car in front of it. He turned to Ellen's mom and said, 'I feel a quietness already.'

Her mom said it seemed a dry place.

Cole said, 'What's that?' like he always did, and when Ellen looked down at his finger, he tickled her chin like he always did. But everything else was strange.

A man named Suresh came running down a hill after someone in the general store phoned him. He was wearing yellow shorts and a yellow T-shirt. Cole was going to start wearing yellow, too, because yellow was the only colour monks were allowed to wear. Suresh hugged everyone and walked them up to the tipi Cole was to live in. He said the monks lived in one corner of the property, the nuns in another. There was an area in Peace Hills for families and one for singles.

It was hot like late afternoons get in the summer – except it was only the beginning of June. Andy was puffing and trying not to show it. Suresh said the most important thing to understand was the omnipresence of poison oak. Ellen was dying to see Cole's tipi. All those times they'd pretended to be Indians, and now he was going to be living like one. But when Suresh held open the flap for them to step through, there was just dirty white canvas and a sleeping bag on a piece of foam. A see-through five-gallon water jug. A meditation bench. A couple of

milk crates with stuff inside. A kerosene lantern. She'd pictured herself spending a lot of time here with Cole, and also
going to see movies with him.

'Hope the nuns get a better colour,' Ellen's mom said. 'Yellow makes women look sallow.'

Suresh said it actually made them look very good. 'I don't
mean pretty,' he said. 'I mean sunny. I mean it suits them.'

Andy looked a little peeved. 'I just don't know sometimes if
you're ready,' Ellen heard him say to her mom later. Ellen and
her mom and Andy were stomping down the pegs for the tent
they'd bought in Salt Lake City. It was a fancy tent with a zip-
on 'room' where Ellen was to sleep. They were going to live in
the tent in the family section all summer because so many people were moving to Peace Hills that there weren't enough cab-
ins and tipis for all of them.

'I'm still not completely used to God,' Ellen's mom said
when they'd moved the air mattresses and pillows and sleeping
bags inside and were flopped down on top of them. Ellen was in
her zip-on room, listening by default. 'You've got to remember
He's pretty new to me. But I think I really, truly love Him.'

They'd been at Peace Hills for more than a month before
Swami Sananda returned from a speaking tour on the eastern
seaboard. He wore a big watch and something that looked like
a yellow sari. The colour signified that he was a monk, like
Cole. Ellen's mom was very impressed that Swami Sananda
was from old money in San Francisco. She said he could be
doing a lot of things besides living in a cabin but still had followed his calling.

Swami Sananda gave people spiritual names, like Prem and
Lakshmi. He would meditate on whether they were ready for
the new names, and if so, which best suited their spiritual
quest. Ellen's mom and Andy were anxious to earn theirs. Ellen
was scared the swami would take her real name away and call

her something like Devi or Radha in this big ceremony where she'd have to stand in front of the entire village and chant Hindu stuff.

Someone had started drywalling and plastering the temple, but there was still plywood on the floor. There were field flowers on the altar and a big picture of the guru. Ellen sat cross-legged finding faces in the knots while Swami Sananda went on about the light inside you and the principle of daily enlightenment and the four steps to spiritual cleansing. As far as she could tell, all you had to do was think good thoughts all the time and you would become distilled – he used that word a lot – into the essence of *nirvana*. Ellen had never 'watched' her thoughts before. She tried it for a while but she was as bored as a babysitter. Her mom and Andy seemed to be getting a lot out of the talk, though. They sat behind her and whenever Ellen turned around to look at them they were holding hands and looking at each other like they were looking into a mirror.

Finally, the Swami stopped talking and asked a man named Gopal to play the harmonium. Ellen could hear her mother's thin *Om mani padmi hum* and Andy's more certain chant.

After, the Swami passed Ellen a hot paper cup. 'Do you like chai?'

'No.'

'Do you have any yearnings you'd like to share?'

'No, I'm not working right now. But I was a paper girl before.'

'Oh my goodness, you charming girl. I meant is there anything of a spiritual nature you'd like to discuss?'

She wondered how big and squishy and white his bum was under all that yellow cloth and if he farted a lot. Then she got a little scared and felt her face go red. 'Are you a mind-reader?'

'No, little one.'

She was tempted to say, 'Oh well, better luck next lifetime,' but she didn't because her mom would kill her and also she was going to wind up laughing with spit shooting out. 'Do you know who I am?'

'A seeker, like all of us.'

'No, see, I come from Canada. So you don't know one thing about me.' She'd never said anything like this before and didn't know it could feel so good in such a goose-pimpled way.

'I can see your aloneness. You must ask God to help release your sorrow so that the poison will stop.'

She tried to push it back by putting her hand over her mouth but she was already laughing pretty loud and she knew right away it was going to be an amazing laugh because her stomach hurt and she just wanted it to keep hurting more. She laughed even after Swami Salami walked away and she knew she was going to be in trouble.

That night, when they were back at the tent and the lecture about how she'd acted like she was maybe eight years old seemed like it was winding down, Ellen's mom said, 'You know, just for a second, I thought how nice it was to see you smile.'

Andy said, 'But you used it as a weapon.'

'That's right, honey,' Ellen's mom said. 'Like a chisel.'

And Andy told her the other children were to stay away from her, at least until she got a handle on her negativity. Swami's orders.

It wasn't like there was anyone around to talk to anyway. Cole could only come and eat with them on Sunday nights because monks were supposed to stay away from the family areas. When Cole wasn't working in the print shop, he was expected to spend a lot of time meditating with the other monks or by himself.

Some afternoons Ellen went to the building her mom and Andy were fixing up and turning into a pottery studio. It had electricity, and Ellen would lie on a piece of carpet and listen to the radio. She'd wake up sweaty. She'd answer things her mom asked about: yeah, she took a bucket bath; yeah, she saw that yellow bird again; yeah, she guessed she felt better after her nap.

Her dad had told her to be sure and phone collect with the new address. She'd waited two weeks and then three, and then told herself she'd forgotten, but her mother remembered and made her call. Ellen walked over to the general store to use the pay-phone. When her dad asked what Peace Hills was like, Ellen said she had a lot of freckles from the sun. She told him he'd like it because it was a very historic area, that she'd seen the places where they'd used hydraulic hoses to drill away the hills with water. She told him there was gold everywhere, even now.

'So do you have a house?' he'd said.

She decided against using the word 'tent'. 'A little one.'

'What's it look like?'

'Well, it's only got one bedroom but there lot's of light and we're getting a bigger place soon. And I get the bedroom all to myself.'

She could hear him crying on the phone. Well, she couldn't hear it. She could tell by the silence that he was crying.

'Daddy? I kind of wish someone would come and get me.'

He didn't say anything. 'How's Cole, then?' he said after a while. 'Does he have a girlfriend out there?'

When she repeated what their dad had asked, Cole snorted. 'You should have told him I'm spending a lot of time with this awesome brunette, Kali. A real goddess.' Cole stopped smiling. 'I shouldn't have said that. She's very powerful.'

'I don't get it. I thought you turned into a monk.'

'She destroys fools. I pray to lots of gods, but Kali's right up there. You know what's funny? I already know I'm going to spend my whole life in service.'

'You're going into the army? Are you going to tell Mom?'

'Hey, what gives?'

She'd clasped her hands and punched him in the arm as hard as she could.

She talked about it one night years later when her mother came to Labrador for a visit. Ellen and her mom tried to go snow-shoeing that afternoon but it was too cold, so they'd come home and napped instead. When they woke up, it was already dark and both of them felt switched around so they decided to forget about supper and just have a glass of wine instead. Ellen said, 'Did you ever think what it was like for me, moving to California like that?' She'd imagined the line many times but when she actually said it, it came out nasty.

Her mother wasn't hurt, though. Oh yes, she'd been worried sick about Ellen, especially after that last visit with her dad. Her mom had tried to make up for it by staying on in Montreal for a couple of days, just the two of them, didn't she remember?

Ellen said, 'There was that shop that only sold buttons and that place with all the Ukrainian Easter eggs.'

'Don't forget Andrés Segovia,' her mother said.

He was an old man with a big round head who had taken forever to shuffle-step over to his stool in the middle of the stage. He had played and played complicated songs that got boring after a while. When he managed to push himself up off the stool everyone was up on their feet shouting 'Bravo, Mae-stro!', including Ellen's mom, who was smiling at her and also saying 'Come on' to Ellen. Ellen did stand up because it felt strange being the only one down low. But she didn't call out 'Bravo' or 'Encore' because she thought if she did maybe some-one would notice her and make her get up on the stage.

'Didn't you love that night?' her mother said.

'It was long.'

'It was your special night,' her mother said. 'I wanted you to see the light shining from him.'

'But it was your music.'

'He was a genius. He could say things.'

'I thought you were just dragging me along so you could go.'

'You were a smart kid, but you didn't always think so good.'

What Ellen wants to know is why she hadn't had any sense of what her mother was thinking. There was nothing cryptic about her father standing on that platform, crying. Which was what had made Ellen so mad at him for such a long time: if she knew he didn't care, she could just say, 'My dad was a jerk.' She'd be able to tell people, perhaps not casually, but without any great pangs, that when she was twelve her mother wanted to take her to a commune at the very same time her father wanted to put her in foster care. It would be much like the other stories she tells about her family, a bit awful but not absolutely terrible. Except this one's more complicated. There's the love her mother didn't know how to show, and then there's her father. His pain was to offer Ellen a love that couldn't help her, and hers was to take it.

✎ Little Spanks ✎

There's a trick to these storms – they come when Lenny is on the road. My husband is a dentist. He has the main office here, and a smaller one in Arnold's Cove he goes to every Tuesday. There are two plastic chairs in the waiting area. The door next to one of them opens onto the room with the drill. The other room has a sofa-bed and TV, one of those big braided rugs covering some of the tiles. He stays over when the weather is down. Gracie does too. I can't prove it, because Lenny's only excuse for staying is that the roads are bad. But it's perfect – he won't lie to me. He doesn't have to. You don't take chances in the winter around here. Five people died the week before Christmas, a car and a tractor-trailer. Better to wait it out, that's why Lenny always takes an extra shirt with him.

I see them, the bar in the middle of the bed making them arch like dolphins, the TV on, the smell of burning teeth.

Yesterday I told him he could have her all the time. I meant it as a gift mostly. Also, I wanted him to remember me just long enough to tell me. I need his words, need him to say he is for her.

'What are you doing to me?' That's all he says before he swings for his lunch bag and goes out the door. He slips on ice at the bottom of the driveway and almost falls. He rights himself, stands perfectly still, as if he's reading the graffiti on the hill across the harbour. He turns and nods to Sam next door and clomps away.

Gracie is my cousin. She has a beautiful ass, the kind meant for love bites and little spanks. Her laugh stays with you the way the taste of licorice clouds your mouth. Gracie paints lupins and skeletons. She also does icebergs for the tourists. That's how she gets by – they pay whatever she asks. Greenish white, streaked with purple, big orange splotches for the puffins' feet. She used to sell fishing scenes, the houses and stages all tilting toward the waves. But it's the icebergs people want. She says if she did one right, instead of for money, it would be dark grey against black water. So grey you couldn't really see it, except you'd know it was there.

The top floor of her house and most of the second are closed off in the winter. The rest is always cold. She never gets her wood cut in time to dry properly and her electric heaters are a joke. She's hung moose antlers over her woodshed. They're covered in polka dots. She figures Nish Collins down the road will hang her cat in revenge one day.

We were laughing drunk, putting on lipstick in the bathroom of the Star of the Sea hall when I told her. Kissing in his car, wriggling. That was a few years ago.

'You?' she'd said. 'You?'

Lenny was in Quebec City at a dentists' convention. Every time I woke up, Herbert's hand was still on my hip. I decided I would tell Lenny as soon as he got back.

But when I went to St. John's to get him at the airport he told me he'd been thinking we should get a dog, that he'd do all the work.

Herbert phoned once after that, and I went over in the afternoon. We didn't say hello, just took our clothes off in the living room. After, he said we could never be together again. He told me he had a cavity and didn't want Lenny's drill to slip. Then serious: 'It's not me you're after. The two of you go walking, and everyone stops to watch you pass.'

'What's this then?' I say. He shakes his head. We kiss, one little breath after another.

When it blows, this place twitches and hums. Downstairs is not so bad, though the wind sucks at the stove damper like a tongue on a chalky peppermint. Upstairs, the bathroom fan clunks and the window in the front bedroom whines against the frame, even with rags pushed into the crack. There are strange easy moments between gusts, until another one pushes at the house. The outside walls move then, just a little. The water in the toilet sloshes back and forth.

I usually pour a couple of rums to mute the din. Some nights I reach under the bed and pull out the fiddle Lenny's uncle, Albert, left him. I let it shriek until my elbow aches.

I've tried to learn as much as I can from Wilf Stokes. He comes for a visit sometimes, has one small nip before he'll play. His fingers mash the strings.

'It's like this,' he says, but I can never see what he's doing. He listens with his eyes closed and doesn't say anything when I'm finished. One time he said, 'You'll be good enough one of these days.'

I tutor his granddaughter, Jacinta, in exchange. Wilf says the more French and stuff she knows, the easier it will be for her to get work on the mainland. He says this as if Jacinta's leaving has already been arranged, although she's only in grade nine. She's hopeless, but sweet. Every time we meet, she tells me I have pretty hair. A couple of times her father has asked me to phone in an order for his hardware store to a company in Quebec. Plastic flowers for graves, Gore-Tex jackets, ski-doo parts. I tell him my French isn't that good but he says never mind, it's better than his.

I want to know when Gracie stopped thinking Lenny was boring. She used to roll her eyes when he talked, or lean back and let her head rest on the top of the chair. He hangs the tea towel over the oven door and sits at the table. I know he is comparing us. Our gumption, our tantrums. Me in a nightgown, her. The light in the kitchen is too bright. The dough sticking to my hands makes my skin itch. If I could, I'd make snowflakes all day long, each one lacy, cut with very sharp sewing scissors. The secret to a good one is to leave only tiny wisps of paper holding it together. It should be mostly air.

'Play for me,' he says.

The smell of the bread is strong even in the living room. I stand by the window, don't notice how the frost has blocked it until after I put the fiddle down. Lenny is in the kitchen. I hear the scrape of the oven rack, the soft thuds as he turns the bread out of the pans to cool. He stays in the kitchen until after I fall asleep.

Lenny's hands are too clean. He wears rubber gloves to do the dishes, and heavy cloth ones in the garden. He rubs his hands with lemon after chopping garlic. Lenny wants to be soothing, inoffensive as he pries open his patients' mouths and leans in. He says there is no way to erase the fear, even if the drill didn't make that noise. But his touch is warm. I know some of the wariness leaves as his fingers push down on their cheeks.

'Coca-Cola is stripping them down to the gums,' he says, 'eating through their teeth like dry rot.' At the strip mall last week, he saw a baby with pop in its bottle. He went over and spoke to the mother.

'Right you are,' the woman said, 'but from what I understand, you've got some bad habits of your own to mind.'

When he told me about it, he stared at the clock and said he was sorry. I heard later it was Edith Butt he'd been talking to.

I floss every day. Sometimes I leave the bathroom door open so he'll hear the sound of the thread going pick-pick through my teeth. He doesn't care, he says my breath is good, but I've always thought you should bend a little, show someone you can move in their element with ease.

I phone Gracie. We go to the Pot-Luck, order egg rolls and hamburgers for lunch.

She says, 'He's a lot better than I expected.'

I know Gracie too well, I don't say anything.

'Do you want him back?' she says after Stella pours water in our glasses.

I stay quiet. Gracie picks up my hand. Her fingers jerk and jump. When I look back up to her face, she starts to giggle. I laugh too. A tiny piece of chewed burger lands on her cheek, but she ignores it. There's a steady buzzing, a low beep-beep outside. The lift bridge going up. I brush off her cheek. She leans forward across the table and talks softly.

'How about a three-way?' She wiggles her eyebrows.

'Before bingo or after?' I ask, and now we're bouncing our feet on the floor.

Gracie says, 'Buy me a beer before I piss my pants.'

Last night Lenny stayed away. I dreamt his uncle Albert died all over again. A bunch of us stood around the casket, and every so often someone would say, 'But he just got a job last week. He just got a job.' And that made all of us cry, waves and waves of tears.

Lenny phones in the afternoon. 'I won't be around much for a while.'

'Oh,' I say. And that's it.

Sometimes I wonder what the odds are of shuffling a deck of cards and having them come out in perfect order, the way they are in a brand new pack.

Marge's kitchen has a red kettle, red canisters, even red plastic measuring spoons hung on hooks. Cream yellow walls. She pushes a plate of date squares over to me.

I'm laughing, telling her at least if I ever need a root canal, it won't cost anything. Telling her I expect Gracie to plant my garden for me and feel so guilty she'll weed it for me too.

Marge says, 'That's right, honey, you just let it all out. You just keep going, honey, and work it out of you. You just let it come up.'

The red and white boxes on her gingham tablecloth hurt my eyes.

'Just heave it out of you,' she says.

When I walk home, the kids are shooting down the hill by the cemetery on their magic carpets. They try to run back to the top but their feet kick out and sometimes they slide all the way back down on their backs, the bright plastic scooting ahead of them.

Herbert gets up from the couch to get me another beer, and the floor shakes under his feet. He lives in a thirty-five-foot trailer. The glass I'm drinking out of has a thumbprint on it. He sits at the other end of the couch, staring at the TV. It's on, but the volume's turned down.

'How can I do you?' he says. A car drives into a jungle sunset. We sit there watching. Then he says, 'If it takes the sting away, he didn't get a new woman. You and Gracie just traded places is all.'

'Asshole.'

'Exactly what she would have said.' He's still grinning as I put my boots on. 'But remember it's you I'm wild for, Liz.'

We chose the house for its colour. A yellow that almost passes into orange. The house is the shape of an upended tea crate. Out the windows of what used to be the parlour, you can see over the steel wall built to keep the waves from spilling against the houses when there's weather. The wall is rusting, and the rust bleeds through the snow that's been pasted on by the wind. On a notepad I write, *I do not want to remember this time*. I rip out the page, fold it into a chunky wad and hide it at the back of my underwear drawer.

'I wasn't going to sleep with him,' I tell Marge the next

morning. 'I wasn't going to sleep with him ever again. I just went there.'

'You straighten up,' Marge says. 'You dipped your toes.'

'No,' Gracie says. 'You can't.' Her nostrils flare wide. She's slouched forward with her breasts pushed up under her arms. 'Does Lenny know?'

I want to get pregnant. I want my belly to jump away from my ribs, to flower crazily. If it's a boy, I'll get a sailor suit with baggy knickers made for him.

'I know I'm old,' I tell Gracie.

'Are you asking for him back?'

'People will just keep saying what they've been saying, only they'll have some more to say.'

I want to cross my eyes and stick out my tongue. I want to go tobogganing. I am bursting, restless.

'Have you been careful?' she says.

'Have you?'

'I'm throwing up a little bit,' she says.

It's getting dark out and her kitchen floor is cold. I make her some tea.

Lenny gives me a puppy for Christmas. 'Cuter than I ever was,' he says. The dog cries when there's a gale. He trembles against me and licks my hand.

Lenny takes down the moose antlers hanging above Gracie's shed. She's working on a painting, she's got it in a room on the second floor. She locks the door when she's done for the day. Her stomach is pointy.

We compare stories about getting groceries at Sobeys. She's sure she hears people hissing at her, soft, under-the-breath hisses. I get the *you poor dear* looks.

I have four suitcases and a case of partridgeberry jam in the back of the car. The dog's chin bumps the edge of the window, paws scrabbling the seat. A job lined up in St. John's, at least for a few months, a contract for the government.

I'm leaving the house the way it is for now – blankets on the bed, the curtains up, placemats on the kitchen table. I give my plants to Gracie. She holds my hand and her tears stick in the fuzz on the baby's head, who howls until she feels a nipple on her cheek.

'I'm the one who should be going,' Gracie says.

The way she says it, it's not an apology. Lenny stands with his hands in his pockets. 'At least show her your painting before she goes.'

She shakes her head, and lowers it over the baby. When I pull out of the drive, I feel Gracie's eyes on me, the way you feel an old woman watching you from behind a lace curtain.

'So you'll be leaving us for a while,' Wilf Stokes says, even though I told him a couple of weeks ago. He pats the top of the car. 'Now don't come back from the city with an earring in your nose or any of that.' I smile. He looks up, lets his head tilt and roll as if he's examining each cloud. 'Looks like snow. You'll come right back if it gets messy, won't you.' He hands me a bottle of moose.

'You stay steady,' I say. The violin is in the back seat. I have a feeling I won't play it again for a long time. When I get to the bridge, it's up. I put the car in park and wait. The dog barks after a couple of minutes.

Seven Reasons Why I Am an Ideal Candidate for Rescue

1. It will make me, Osmond Vinnicombe, a better citizen

You should know, my dear Dr Rumper, that I am often overcome by a listless fatigue, a worrisome sense that the future is no more than an extension of the monotony of the moment. I am led to understand the Uplifter engenders an atmosphere of achievement, something that is lacking most pitifully in my life. No doubt this confession will shock you – during our earlier meetings I presented myself as a common man. I told you I am remarkable only in that I am considered finicky and severe. What I did not explain, what I could not then explain, is how I, Osmond Vinnicombe, came to be labelled so cruelly.

The first insult was levied by way of snippish comment on the part of my landlady, one Marla Grandsome, just before she began her unfortunate hospital stay. The circumstances were simple – I had requested she attend to the matter of the fan in the bathroom. It clunked as if a bird were trapped inside and bursting its heart with fear. But really, the hellish noise resulted from the age of the fan and the domination of rust. The woman had the gall to call me finicky (is there any word that hisses more on the tongue?), not caring that the clanking so disturbed me that I had to stop turning on the fan. The switch controlled the light as well, and so I was forced to bathe by candlelight and to shave with no little trepidation.

The term 'severe' has never been applied directly to me. But it is hinted at on my employee evaluation form, which I chanced upon one day in the supervisor's office. Dr Rumper, I'm sure you remember that I am a parking meter-man – no doubt you recall the seven minutes' grace I granted you last

March? Well, imagine my surprise at reading the following: 'Insists Deputy Mayor show identification.' '12-12-00/Phonecall – Handicapped male, snow prevents from returning to vehicle on time, OV issues ticket irregardless'. 'Fines D-Mayor, 3rd complaint, despite briefing.'

I have a job to do and I do it as if there is no other (although in truth that statement does not apply to this week, but we will get to that later). My dedication, however, has gone unrewarded. Hunchbacks are less familiar with disgust, trolls more certain of their welcome.

Dr Rumper, when last we met, you questioned why I had sought you out and told me never to return. But since I had revealed only a sliver of my being, you cannot be blamed for pronouncing me whole. I showed you a new moon, and we both continued on as if it existed independent of its swell of darkness. Forgive me: I withheld; I glossed; I distorted. Permit me one chance at bravery, one more shot at the uncomfortable task of unveiling my scuttling fears. Because, despite what you think, I need help.

As I write, I take a steadying breath and prepare to strip off my pride, my hidden dignity: the two have been my uniform these many years. I hesitate, wondering if you will judge me and find me loathsome. I beg you, good doctor, to hold in check any harshness my confession generates. Understand you are the thread by which I hang.

I must share that which is so repugnant to me, and surely to all. I cannot stall any longer, for the truth is I am overcome by a fascination that cannot be healthy, a bad habit that I cannot break on my own.

It is my ants. I can't leave them alone. Oh, I told the cashier the ant farm was intended for my dear nephew, Wilson. But the truth is I would not let his murderous soul within a quarter-mile of the colony. My heart darted and hummed as I poured the sand into the acrylic walls. The trouble is that now I can't bear to tear myself away from my industrious family. One evening I conducted an experiment with some peanuts, placing them in a pile in one corner. The ants soon had a plan – some got busy enlarging Tunnel 'C' while others swarmed and wrestled their bounty toward the hole. On a whim, I placed a dot of liquid paper on the back of one of the strugglers. And would you believe it, Rumper, that same white-dotted ant (since dubbed Lester) comes out of Tunnel 'D' each evening at exactly 5:17, which is three to five minutes after I arrive home from work?

I am transfixed. My television sits cold and neglected. Supper is a corned-beef sandwich, although I do indulge in tea and fig newtons for dessert. I eat in the recliner, next to the precious abode. I'm pointing out signs of catastrophic change here – let me tell you I once made a decent hash each night and ate it properly at the table with a cross-word for company. Now look at me. I am sliding and unable to stop myself. I've stopped taking the garbage out and laundry has become sporadic. I am falling apart.

Further proof: I have been absent from my Shriners meetings and have received frantic phone calls about the upcoming parade. I'm told my participation is crucial, since many of our men have been felled by influenza. However, I doubt I will go, even though my job year after year has been to drive one of the tiny cars. A coveted role, and one I've enjoyed in the past. But I am not the same man. I find the idea of careering down Water Street doing figure eights and honking that bulbous horn entirely wasteful. No bobbing and weaving for ants, only purpose. Ditto for Osmond Vinnicombe.

But that raises a terrifying question. Just what is my purpose, Rumper?

I'm sure it's clear to you by now that I need at the very least a three-month trial of the Uplifter.

Should you require more encouragement, let me mention I

have not yet filled out my income tax return this year. It also seems a useless exercise. Can't you see, Rumper, that by writing one simple prescription for my well-being, you could stimulate a renewed patriotism? In these difficult times, I'm sure you can see the wisdom in my words.

2. I am choked by remorse

Past stupidities, both glaring and small, leap out at me when I need full rein over my abilities. The result: I have been unable to report to work for seven days. The trouble started innocently enough. Last Thursday morning, I was hurrying to remove a small stain from my tie before dashing out the door to go to work. I performed this chore in the hallway in front of the oval mirror. Perhaps it was my agitation at the thought of being late. Or perhaps it was that rash second cup of coffee. Whatever the reason, I suddenly recalled one of the most terrible events of my childhood. You will likely laugh at what I am about to describe. It involves no bullies holding me by the ankles in the outhouse, no pup slipping under the wheel of a tractor, no bitter memories of an unjustified thrashing. But to my mind, my story is no less damaging.

I broke a chain letter when I was eleven years old. It had circled the world nineteen times in six years. And I, lazy child, did not send the eight requisite postcards to the addresses provided. One was in Rhodesia, I remember that. I picture some poor boy suffering the heat day after day, eagerly checking the mailbox – only to discover no comfort from Newfoundland. I recall tearing the solicitous form letter into bits and lighting them on fire in the bathroom sink. It was the same day I ripped every flimsy page out of my mother's Bible. I was angry at her for some reason – you'd think I would remember why. But it is the chain letter that makes me weep for an innocence I've never known or deserved.

Dr Rumper, all that returned to me last Thursday morning. I ran into the bathroom and heaved the contents of my wretched being. Over the past few days, other instances of my selfishness have come back to me. There are the times I thought about pushing my landlady, the now-deceased Marla Grandsome, down the stairs. Or the Christmas I deliberately crushed nephew Wilson's miniature robot underfoot. Inexcusable, really.

All this means I can no longer be a meter-man. How can I continue to be the arbiter of even the most elemental courtesy and responsibility when I myself am so clearly lacking?

3.   I believe I may be in danger of taking my own life

I suspect these words might surprise you – after all, only last month you deemed me not in need of spiritual assistance, either from analysis or the Uplifter. Your diagnosis was indeed correct, given that until now I have been hiding my deeply interior fears from you. It is no wonder you concluded there was nothing wrong with me (I paraphrase here) that a whirl on a dance floor and a hangover wouldn't fix.

I am a shy man, so shy in fact I've suffered from hemorrhoids for the past three and a half years without seeking professional intervention. I've been too embarrassed to mention this problem to my family doctor. I tell you this so you will understand what desperation has forced me to pen this SOS.

I don't know if you will find a pistol lying in a puddle of gore or a rope groaning under the full weight of my grief. But I do believe this letter will torment you should I suddenly pass on.

4.   A bottle of Scotch

Dr Rumper, let me reassure you lest you think I am a beast. As a measure of my gratitude for your kind ministration of the

Uplifter, I will see that a bottle of your favourite liquor is placed in your deserving hands.

5. My life has been needlessly lonely

The severity for which I am known constrains me in an unbearable solitude. (I sometimes think my presence would be less frightening without my woolly eyebrows. I once spent two agonizing hours trimming them, but the result was uneven.) I have never known the pleasures of friendship. No visitors vie for my affection. No woman has ever so much as run her fingers through my curls.

Surely I don't have to spend my life pining for the impossible. I believe my social awkwardness is no more than a foil, an attempt to fend off any interaction that would expose my ragged inadequacies.

I believe that with the Uplifter working for me, I could at least manage to squeak out a greeting to the neighbours.

Dr Rumper, I want to throw my head back and shriek at ridiculous jokes. I want to catch a baby's eye and hold her enthralled in my gaze. I want to explode with delicious fear as I ask Miss Lilah Farrow to accompany me for a stroll.

There is so much, so much.

6. Very little effort is required on your part

Such a simple thing: you unlock a desk drawer and tear off a prescription form. With a quick flick of your wrist, your illegible scribble leads to my redemption.

7. Others will benefit

The ants have made me humble, have made me realize I am only one dot in a clump of dots. Perhaps no one should care

about Osmond Vinnicombe – an inconsequential man who neither takes from nor gives to his world, a man who was not
noticed during life and who won't be missed after death.

A nothing of a man asking to be seen as at least a slip of a
man.

It's all right, Rumper. I, too, would laugh if only I had the
reserves.

And perhaps that's all I need – a layer of insulation. I do not
expect miracles from the Uplifter, only a moderate uplifting.
Enough to allow me to return to what I had known as my life.
To inspire me to take out the garbage, to gather the strength to
lift the lid of the shoebox where I keep my tax receipts, and
most of all, to get me back on the job. To feel the old thrill on
approaching a parking meter with one minute left. I would
stand there whistling, wondering if the owner would come lop-
ing along and plead for mercy. I used to find the excuses enter-
taining, every driver complaining about being held hostage in
some way – plodding dentists, sweethearts demanding one
more kiss. I enjoyed most their stuttering rage as I pulled out
my pad and clicked on my pen. But lately, these scenes have
inspired only ennui. I am tired of being called heartless and
even more tired of the attempts to charm me in those moments
before I unsnap the pad. I wouldn't care for a hotdog with some
nice onions, would I? I didn't by any chance go to school with
their pop, did I? What a nice watch. Say, what kind of cologne
is that?

Pah. Syrupy words that soon turn to vinegar.

Rumper, give me back my revels, small as they were. Picture
me smiling. How many men are there like me, and how much
do we weigh down the world?

⏑ Ketchup Boy ⏒

Dana is probably going to have an accident because she hasn't slept in any meaningful way for the past three weeks and now she's driving in the dark and in the rain, and nothing seems square. The edges of buildings are more like flashes than lines. Even the blackness – which predominates – is wiggling between her windshield wipers. She's driving to Quidi Vidi Lake to go for a jog, but she keeps forgetting that; she winds up going downtown to Duckworth Street first. And then she misses two turns in a row that would take her where she wants to be, which is the parking lot at the boathouse. She circles back. In St. John's, if you just keep rolling along you'll eventually hit the place you're trying to hit. She parks, and starts running once she's just past the boathouse. It's not raining so hard any more. She tries to avoid the puddles, but some can't be seen. The point of the run is to burn off enough energy so that maybe she'll be able to sleep. It's good to move. Something high up in her spine snaps, and the relief that comes with it makes her feel lucky. Even when it starts to pour, there's a pleasure in allowing her body to steam forward, to actually do something.

Just past the canteen, she sees a tiger squatting beside the path. She understands within a second that it's not really there, which terrifies her even more. I am more tired than a Texan pig, she thinks. Which doesn't make any sense, but it's fun. I am more tired than an old shoelace. I am more tired than a prairie dog with dentures. Than a surgeon with Epstein-Barr. I am more tired than a boot factory.

She gets to the car and home in one piece. She takes the right roads and she stops when she's supposed to stop, signals when she turns, and most importantly doesn't kill any old women who might be in a hurry to cross the road because their hands are cold and wet and raindrops are rolling right inside their grocery bags.

A salad. Herbal tea. A bath and then bed. The shock of sleep. This is the plan.

Except someone knocks on the door while she's rinsing the lettuce. The election is next week, it's probably Dana's MHA. She stays by the sink, flicking leaves, even though whoever is at the door can see her. She pretends she's deaf. The knocking continues. She wipes her hands on a dishtowel, and walks into the living room where it is dark and therefore no one can stare at her. She sits down for a second. Fuck. Maybe it's someone coming to view the house. That happened the other night at suppertime – she answered a knock and there was a couple on the step with an agent, waiting to come in. They'd set up the appointment the day before, they said. But Dana hadn't received notice. She had clothes on the bathroom floor and dishes on the counter. She shouldn't have – she knew the viewings often happened with less than an hour's notice. But she'd been so achy that morning. She'd sat at the kitchen table with a cup of coffee staring at the dogberry tree instead of picking everything up before she went into the office. Some mornings she's washed the floors before going in. Because she needs to sell the house fast. She takes possession of the new house in three weeks, which is why she needs to pay attention to first impressions. Which is also why she's had insomnia. The inevitability of paying two mortgages, two heat bills, and two insurance bills keeps her mind grinding. The down payment for the new home is on her line of credit, with interest charges ticking away. If she has to cover the costs of two houses for more than two months, she's doomed. It's the neighbourhood that's getting in the way of selling her house. That's what the real estate agent says. People who like the place keep driving by at night and seeing police cars on the block. Which is exactly why she's moving. She's not afraid of the neighbours, but she is ready for less domestic excitement.

It's Earle at the door, the boy who lives down the street. 'Miss Dana, I have to borrow some t-p.' He has his head back, with blood coming through his hands. Dana pulls him into the hall. He keeps his head tipped up, but his eyes swoop up, across, across. 'Nice house, miss.'

'Where are your shoes?' By which time she's got him at the kitchen table with her fingers pinching the bridge of his nose. He's rammed most of a Kleenex up a nostril and she's saying, 'Get those socks off. And don't talk, don't tell me anything.'

But he chatters, his voice strangled and happy. Was he ever bleeding a lot and Holy God it was a lot of blood. He was in the shed when he could feel it start, and then his nose turned into a hose. Hose nose, that's what it was, hey. It started pumping so much blood that the guys made him go home.

He takes out the Kleenex and puts his fingers right back on his nose. Dana gets a pair of socks and a face cloth from upstairs. He hesitates, puts the socks on after she nods.

She wets the washcloth. 'Stick it up there,' she says. She picks up the tissue by the white part and drops it into the garbage can. 'Where's your mom?'

His mom made him a birthday cake last week, and it was excellent.

'What's your phone number?'

They don't have a phone. They used to have a phone. But they don't have a phone this month.

She gets him some orange juice. It's hard for him to swallow, with his nose pinched. His mom gave him thirty bucks, too, right? But then she was playing the machines and someone stole her purse, which was down on the floor at the bottom of her stool. All she did was take her foot off the strap for half a second, and there it was, gone, with his birthday money inside. 'She's still going to give it to me,' he says. 'Next month.' And then a smile shines his eyes. 'She probably spent it on the machines, right?'

'Keep your jaw still for a while.'

They wait. Earle always gets a nosebleed when it's hot like this.

'But it's raining,' she says. 'I wouldn't call this hot.'

'It's not shivery rain, though, right?'

Earle used to have a Game-Boy. Does she have a computer? He wants to get a DVD player. He likes to write letters to people who are famous, such as one time the Incredible Hulk. And another time Hulk Hogan. He likes that word. People named Tulk should change their name. He knows a Tulk. Jimmy Tulk is in his shop class. Jimmy Hulk.

That would be Hulk Jimmy in the phone book, Dana says.

'Hulk Jimmy.' His body shakes with the funniness of it. 'Hulk Earle.'

'Earle Tulk.'

'Earle Sullivan. I'm Earle Sullivan.'

'I know,' she says. 'I'm joshing you.'

He stares at her.

'I'm just kidding you. Teasing,' she says.

'Where are you from?'

'Your mom,' Dana says. 'She had to be telling the truth.'

He says sure he knows that, and does she have a computer or not?

And Dana looks right at him and says no. 'Try now,' she says.

Earle pulls the washcloth away from his face. A long clot comes with it.

'Oh,' he says, 'that's chokey.' And then his hand goes up to his nose again and there's just as much blood as ever. 'For fuck's sake,' he says.

'Hey,' she says. And gets up to put the lettuce back in the fridge and wipe up the dishes. Since the house was listed, she's been drying them and putting them away instead of leaving them in the drainer. Earle is quiet, watching. 'You know,' she says when she's done, 'I have to eat something. I was going to have a piece of cheese but I can't now because my stomach's gone off.' It's the blood and the fatigue – lately she gets huge hunger pangs that turn into nausea within about five minutes if she doesn't do anything about them.

'So have some scrambled eggs,' he says. 'and I'll be your ketchup bottle.'

'Gross,' she says. But she's giggling. What did he have for supper?

He shrugs. 'Stuff.' He says he can taste the blood running back down and what if he faints?

She tells him not to be silly; it's just a nose bleed.

Dana has collected the best of the magazines and brought them back to Earle. Car racing, mountain climbing, snowboarding, *Readers' Digest* because he'll probably like 'Laughter, the Best Medicine'.

The ER nurse had said they should figure on a four, maybe a five-hour wait. A lot of babies in with spiked temperatures tonight, the pneumonia season is off to a tremendous start. The nurse said Earle should just tell that nasty nosebleed to stop right now so that he can go home. 'Willpower,' she says to Dana. 'It actually works.'

That was at nine-thirty. Now it's eleven-fifteen. Two toddlers are standing together holding each other's faces. They get a kiss in before two mothers, germ-fear making them look angry, swoop the kids away. Babies are crying, sleeping, sucking, cowboy-riding on knees, sticking their hands into their dads' mouths. A teenaged Goth girl sits alone, holding her stomach. A boy about Earle's age has cut some fingers. His mother makes him lie down across the seats with his arm up in the air. There's a smaller boy sitting right next to Earle who looks to be all right. He holds his father's hand very tightly.

Earle keeps pressure on his nose. Dana holds the snowboarding magazine open so that he can see it.

'Turn,' he says every two seconds. 'Turn.'

Aren't the pictures cool? Does he want her to read an article to him? He shakes his head. 'God, I haven't showered yet,' Dana says. She hasn't even rinsed her face, which is tight and dry with dried sweat. She feels pretty good otherwise. There's a pain in her neck like she's going to get a migraine if she's not careful, but otherwise she's okay. If anything, she feels impossibly lucid.

'You stink,' Earle says. His fingers are still holding his nose.

She is proud of him for using irony. They walk down the hall to get him a Pepsi and a straw.

Earle's skin is a strange white. It's not at all comforting that it is the same colour as the day she saw him in the street and asked if he wanted an old ghetto blaster. It wasn't much of an offering – the motor on the cassette player whirred and ground so loudly that it wasn't worth playing any more. Earle ran home with it, and then came back an hour later to say he was going to put it in his window so all his friends down on the street could hear it, and did he mention thank you. Dana saw his mother sitting on her steps not long after that, and Mrs Sullivan had said hello.

Had nodded hello with a cigarette in her mouth, to be accurate.

Dana has an idea. They should call the police and ask them to pop over to the Sullivans' to explain where Earle is. Then Mrs Sullivan can come up to the hospital and not be worrying.

'The police?' Earle says. 'I didn't do anything.'

No, even better, she'll get a friend to go over. That's what she'll do.

She waits until he goes to the washroom. He comes back with a paper towel held to his face. He'd pulled out the cotton ball the nurse had given him and everything seemed fine for a minute. His eyes have welled up with tears. He's dizzy and his mom and dad are going to kill him. He's thirsty like crazy and his butt hurts and his arm's sore and –

Dana hands him more cotton balls from the paper bag the nurse gave them when they signed in and tells him to boogie back to the washroom and get some more cotton up there. When he comes back, she gets some hot chocolate for him out of a machine. And a big oatmeal cellophane cookie, which he says he can't swallow with his nose plugged.

She wakes Gary up, so right off the bat the call goes poorly. 'Just take the kid home,' he says. 'It's just a stupid nosebleed.'

She tells him it's been going for almost five hours. Can Gary go over now?

It's almost midnight, Gary says. He doesn't have any clothes on. He doesn't know these people. Why aren't they looking for their kid – if they were so worried they would have called the Constabulary, and then the cops would have called the hospital and everything would be straightened up.

'Gary?' Dana says. 'He's only 11. Just do it. You have to.'

'Dana?' he says in that soft way he has when he's going to say something that will set her off. 'I thought we just broke up.'

She goes just as quiet. 'It's non-negotiable. I have to work tomorrow.' She tells him she'll call him back in half an hour if there's still no sign of Mrs Sullivan at the hospital.

All she'd said to him was that she was ready to start dating other men. He'd accepted that, wished her luck, and they'd held each other in the usual way that night. In the morning, they both said they'd slept well, and agreed that must mean it was a good decision. Gary started packing and Dana listed the house, her house, because change was good. 'I have to get out of this neighbourhood,' she told people. The spitting, the yelling, the inertia of unemployment.

A thousand times, she's told herself she's got to stop calling Gary. She keeps promising she won't do it again.

Dana has to get out of here. She can't take anything else on.

The emergency room is still humming. Dana hears a mother holding a baby ask the nurse how much longer, and the nurse says just keep listening for your name to be called. The mother nods, wipes away tears, and smiles with embarrassment.

Earle managed to get the cookie down. He looks half-sedated. 'Come here,' she says, and pulls his head against her arm. 'I'll hold your nose.'

She wonders if he has lice. She wonders if she's pinching too hard.

He's asleep. She slouches down so that she can put her own head back against the top of the chair back. She sleeps.

A baby makes the air go stiff with frustration. The father is almost waltzing. The baby is invisible to Dana – all she can see are pink blankets in the father's arms. Her watch reads 12:12. She's been out for five, maybe six minutes. Her fingers are still clamped across Earle's nose. Could she at least sleep for fifteen minutes? Could she not wake up to the sounds of human discomfort, the crying, the mauling of Styrofoam cups, the hiss of the PA system, coins twitching in pockets? Could Gary do something without always making it clear she owes him? Could he just come and get his couch so that she can stop worrying about what she'll do without one? Could he come over to the hospital and maybe suggest something she should do with the boy leaning against her arm, the boy who is wearing her sneakers because he ran over to her house in stocking feet in the rain?

She really had tried to return this boy to his mom. On the way to the hospital, they'd gone to his house to see if anyone was home. But when they went inside – Earle's key on a loop through his belt – there was still no one there. 'Not even one of your sisters?' Dana had said, and made him go upstairs and check. Inside the house, it was clean. The smell of cigarettes, but no dishes in the sink. The kitchen chairs pushed in, place-mats wiped. She opened the fridge. Two loaves of white bread, and three bottles of beer. Some condiments. A slab of bologna.

Earle came down and said nope, nobody around.

'Where do they go?' Dana had asked, but there was no answer.

She shifts Earle so that he's sitting straight up, tells him she has to go pee when his eyelids flutter. Her arm is stiff from holding his nose. What kind of mother would she be?

Gary picks up without saying hello. 'Dana?' he says. 'I'm trying to sleep.'

'You didn't go over.'

'Dana?' he says. 'I'm going to have to go unlisted. I'm telling you now so you won't be surprised.'

'Who is she?'

'So I'm going now, all right?'

'I'm okay. You don't get that I'm okay.'

There's a long wait. 'I just dozed off,' he says finally.

'I'm so jealous. I really, really am.'

'In fifteen seconds, I'm hanging up.'

'I'm still at the hospital with this kid.'

There's another wait.

'What am I supposed to do?' There is a scream within her words. But she's in public right now – restraint is easy.

'Okay, sweetheart, I'm sending nice things your way.' And then the click, the Gary click.

She should have put some mats in the washing machine before heading for the hospital. The house is grungy again. Every viewer leaves a trail of some sort. People leave blinds pulled up, or the back gate open, and they're forever knocking the shampoo bottle into the claw foot bathtub. She wishes she had more exciting prescriptions for them to suss out in the medicine cabinet. Why did she buy the new house without selling the old one first? She wishes she could stay where she is. Everything's messed up. She'd gone back to Gary after going on a couple of dates and told him maybe she didn't want to see other men. But he said he was great with their new set-up – he could love her without any residue.

Will Earle's family notice that someone's been in their house? Did she close the fridge door?

Earle is awake, feet up on the edge of the seat, arms folded.

'You're not holding your nose,' she says.

'I was going to start walking home.'

'Is there haemophilia in your family?'

He doesn't know the word. 'Where's my mom?'

'I mean, maybe you're a bleeder.'

'I know where Dad's to. He's at the Peter Easton, playing darts.'

Dana had seen the father just a couple of days ago, buying a twelve-pack at the corner store. Were they already out of toilet paper? 'Do you think maybe it's stopped? Because we could go home then.'

He shrugs.

'I'm from Ontario,' she says. 'I can't handle this.'

He doesn't remove the cotton, and she decides that's a good idea. She can't take another disappointment. Probably neither can he. They move closer to the TV, even though the volume's turned off.

Dana tries to calculate whether she has enough room on her credit card for a couch. The new house is expensive – it's right in the yuppie middle of the downtown heritage revolution. She'll need a couch of some sort, except that she's already going to put the roof repair and the double mortgage bills on her card.

I am in crisis, she thinks. But the disgusting part is how mundane it is. Two houses, a break-up, so what? 'I'm never going to sleep, am I?' she says, but Earle keeps his eye on the screen. A motorcycle is jumping over a bus. It's a commercial for something.

The doctor is suspicious. Is Dana the mother? Then who is she? Why isn't the mother here? 'Did someone hit you?' he asks Earle, who shakes his head. 'Does anyone hit you?' the doctor says. Earle shakes his head.

The doctor is the kind of person who stands very close. He's maybe thirty-five, but there are bags under his eyes. Maybe he always works nights. At least Dana had remembered to throw some water on her face the last time she was in the washroom. The doctor wants to know what Earle had for breakfast, for lunch, for supper. Earle takes his time, resting between answers. Toast, a tuna sandwich, pea soup. Does Earle get these nosebleeds all the time? Earle nods yes.

'Let's see here,' the doctor says, tugging on the cotton wad with tweezers. 'Okay, well no trouble getting your blood to clot.' Dana looks away. 'How's it feel?' he asks Earle.

Earle says it's okay.

'I'd say it stopped a good while ago.' They have to sit there in the examining room for another fifteen minutes, just to be sure.

'It hurts to look at things,' Earle says.

Dana says that's just because he's super-tired.

The doctor comes back in forty-five minutes and says everything looks good and can he speak to Dana alone for a second.

'Should I report the boy?' he asks.

'I'm sorry?'

'We have a social worker on duty. Shall I go get her?'

Dana stares.

The doctor asks has she seen any evidence? Do they hit him, yell at him? 'I think he's anaemic – I want some tests done.'

'Don't do that,' Dana says. 'Don't take him away.'

'I have a responsibility. At the very least, that blood vessel's going to have to be cauterized sometime soon.'

'I'm only a neighbour. And it's 3 a.m.' Her voice is going to crack.

'Where are his parents?' the doctor says. But he's really saying what kind of a life is it?

She almost says that's exactly why she's moving, to not have to think about questions like that all the time. 'Give me your card,' she says. 'I'm going to take him home.'

In the car, Dana tells Earle she's scared driving. She's so bushed she doesn't know if she'll see anything bad out there.

'Like what?' he says. Headless moose? Ghosts in the cemetery?

'That doctor is a good man,' she says.

They pull into an all-night McDonald's. Earle wants to eat inside, but she says, no, she has to work in a few hours, so it's going to have to be drive-through. He gets through two hamburgers and a milkshake before they get to their street.

She walks him to the door. 'I can't leave until your parents come down. What's your mom's name again?'

Earle says Ruth. There's a song in Dana's head: Wake up, little Ruthie, wake up.

He knocks and knocks and nobody opens the door. 'Why can't I just use my key?'

'Because I have to see these people,' she says.

❧ An Apology ❧

The first day of the trial will be the hardest. Gerard Lundrigan arrives at the courthouse exactly one hour early, at nine o'clock. Even then the TV cameras are waiting, although they're not allowed inside the courtroom. He sits in that dark sanctuary, testing his chair. It will do. He's brought along the Graham Greene book he forgot to return to the library. But he can't read about the whisky priest, not just yet. Gerard makes sure the buttons on his blue cardigan are done up right. He holds the book open so it will look like he's doing something. Outside the tall windows, what looks to be the start of a March storm. He'd forgotten what it was like here. The wind is taking anything it can find. There's a good chance that by noon all of St. John's will be clamped in ice. Or it will be sunny, or raining, or snowing. You never know about this place, he does remember that. He thinks about his pup back in Ontario, and how it likes to nose through the snow. It would like it here, especially rolling in landwash after chasing gulls.

The jurors look nervous as they walk in. One woman giggles when she bumps into a chair on the way to the jury box, and her face stays red for a full hour. The other jurors' eyes swivel over the oak and mahogany scrollings, the ancient picture of the Queen, the thin, bunned judge in her red-sashed blue robe. A sheriff's officer walks around with one hand pressed to his ear piece, the other clamped at his hip to keep the keys on his belt from jingling. Two more sheriff's officers flank Gerard, tapping their fingers against their thighs. There can be trouble on the first day, apparently, scenes. The lawyers look edgy and clear their throats a lot. Gerard isn't sure how many spectators there are – he won't let himself look back. But there are eyes on him, of course – he can feel them. And he can see the jurors studying him. They've relaxed a bit, are sitting more deeply in their chairs. Not one of them looks like a leader. Not one of them looks to be well-studied. Only one man wears a tie. There's even a girl in jeans, chewing gum. They listen hard as the crown prosecutor outlines his case. During the preliminary inquiry, he'd been soft-spoken, methodical. Now he is playing to the jury, and there is insincerity and filth coming out his mouth. Absolute filth.

You're probably nervous, ladies and gentlemen of the jury. I know you are because I myself am nervous right now and I've been at this racket for a long time now. But there's no need to worry. All you have to do is sort through the facts, and I believe those facts are very clearly set out. You are the judge of the facts and as such, you will hear direct testimony that Brother Lundrigan beat little boys. Sodomized little boys. Ejaculated in their mouths as they gagged and struggled.

I know these are shocking things to say, sickening things to say. You probably wish you hadn't had breakfast. All I can say is get used to it, because you're going to hear about it from eleven different men over the course of the next six weeks or so.

Most of the jurors suction their arms across their stomachs and keep them there all morning. Gerard sits very tall and looks straight ahead.

The afternoon is better. The weather has settled somewhat. The first witness is called – the lead investigator from the Royal Newfoundland Constabulary. All he does is show a videotape of the orphanage, a long, long tape showing every room and closet and corridor and shed. The police shot the film before the wrecking ball knocked the place in on itself. There is the chapel, just as Gerard remembers it. The classrooms. The sleeping quarters. The gym. The old garden grounds. And so on, and on and on. All shot poorly, shakily, with bad lighting. But the courtroom has been darkened and therefore no one is staring at Gerard.

When the first complainant takes the stand, Gerard absorbs every word. He remembers the boy well. The one who'd wanted so badly to be on the gymnastics team but was disqualified because he failed math every year. He'd been a big boy then. Now he has the look of a withered drunk. Ridiculous in a burgundy velvet jacket. Soft-spoken – the judge doesn't ask the man to speak up nearly enough. He didn't get that mumbling habit from his time at the orphanage. They'd taught pride there. Pride and decency and right-living.

The fellow goes on for hours about how terrible the orphanage was, how he and his younger brother would steal buns and hide them in the little barn for the times when they couldn't sleep for hunger. How they got in trouble just for sitting still, and worse beatings when they actually did anything bad. How Bro. Lundrigan was the worst one for the strap, especially with the boys in his dorm. How he wouldn't tolerate any illness and wouldn't let a boy go to the sickroom even if he'd thrown up all night. How Bro. Lundrigan would toss any boy who wet the bed into the swimming pool, no matter the time of year. How if he saw a boy crying for any reason, he'd rub soap in the child's eyes so he'd have something to screech about.

Gerard wants to speak. It's physically painful not to be able to respond, acid burning his gut. But since he won't be testifying for at least a month, he's started a notebook outlining every single point he disagrees with, numbering each in case it will help his lawyer.

23) No child ever went hungry in my care.

24) The strap had nothing to do with me. Blame the era, not the man. Do you think your disobedience made me happy – do you think I liked it?

25) I remember personally taking you to the sickroom on at least two occasions.

26) Re: soap – whatever are you talking about?

'Make him stop watching me,' the first complainant says to the judge the fifth morning he's on the stand. The prosecutor has just started in on the buggery allegations. On the fire escape, one night. In the barn, many times. Many, many times. The witness's voice cracks. The judge orders a break.

117) The disgusting thing you allude to – where would I even have gotten the idea? What about my vows? Why would I do such a thing? You brought me here to watch your sickening tears and listen to you say these revolting things?

Gerard is thankful for his lawyer, who establishes in one efficient afternoon of cross-examination that the complainant has a long criminal record, including theft. He'd also attacked a man in a bar with a broken bottle. That's the kind of low-life he is. In and out of mental hospitals, with children spat out across northern Ontario like bits of gristle, and ex-wives lining up to get restraining orders.

The next witness is a real crowd-pleaser. Makes the jury smile as he remembers stringing chestnuts to play conkers. As he describes skinning his shins against the rough concrete of the swimming pool. The time Bro. Superior came in for breakfast one morning dressed like Charlie Chaplin and kept pretending to fall off his chair. What it was like riding the hay wagon into St. John's and seeing all those mesmerizing lights and the houses where you could look in the windows at the moms and dads and pops and nannies and little kids sitting right nice and sweet at the table.

He has them all right. Even the judge looks choked up. And then less than half an hour later, he goes for a bull's-eye. His face is crazy red and he's dry-sobbing and beating one hand against the top of the witness box and pointing with the other: *That one, that one there. That bastard ruined me for everything. Your Honour, I'd as soon spit on him on his deathbed. That's a monster, that is. Not a man. Left me opened up and bleeding so's I couldn't shit for a week. Bite marks on my neck.*

The judge orders a break.

Gerard has begun to put together some theories. These men are forty-five, fifty. They're all into the booze or the drugs. They've all done time. He knows – it all came out at the preliminary hearing.

They've got something else in common: they've disappointed anyone who ever came into their lives. Including Gerard.

Their fathers were alcoholics or thieves or dead and their mothers were sluts or mad or dead. Now they're men looking to blame, to make someone accountable for their empty spots.

And who better than Gerard? They remember him making them sit on their bleeding hands – as was common in those times – and they want revenge, they want to make him sit on his own bleeding hands and get a taste of himself. They'd do that to a sixty-four-year-old because all they want is this one chance in their lives to give out orders and have someone obey.

So, okay, Gerard is sitting on his hands. They've got him where they want him. They wag their fingers like he used to in math class, and now it's him who can't talk back. It's so straightforward eye-for-an-eye that it's almost comic. Except what they really want is for him to fix their lives and that's something he never, ever could do.

A man is not a mother. A twenty-two-year-old thinks he wants to get away from his slightly aristocratic parents. He thinks he wants to roll up his sleeves, get his hands dirty, serve. And so he does. And at first, God is everywhere. In the wind, in his ear, in the fellowship of the twenty-three-year-olds and the twenty-five-year-olds who also want nothing of society auctions and marriage and cigars. But there are fourteen boys in his charge. Two are just four years old, leggy babies with permanent ropes of snot hanging from their noses. Crying always for Mumma. The teen boys are revolting, with their acne and their smell and their trembling beds as they go at themselves in the dark. The middle ones are better, but still they hang off him, one on one arm, another on his back, another trying to get that one off. *Possums*, he'd called them, but he had to explain: no possums in Newfoundland.

Ripped off. Yes, they were. He always knew that. It wasn't easy for them. But it wasn't easy for him, either. Does anyone ever stop and think what it was like? Up at five-thirty for prayers with the other brothers. Getting the boys up at six and trying to get them to wash. Supervising breakfast. Teaching until four. Gymnastics coaching. Homework supervision. Somewhere in there making time to go over to the teachers' dorm and help out with the bed-bound ancient brothers. Then supervising his dorm, staying up all night if necessary with the croupy boys.

And those annual evaluations with the superior. Always getting on about the filth of the place, about how the boys needed to be pushed to do their chores properly. The lavatory like something out of India. How Bro. Superior wanted things pristine, the way they should be. And how the orphanage should be winning more trophies – how good it was for the boys to be the very best, to show them that adversity could be overcome.

One time Gerard muttered under his breath *Yes, Bro., but what about my needs?* It had struck him as funny – by rights he'd prayed them all away hadn't he? That wasn't so long before he left. He remembers it was a Tuesday, and he'd walked back over to the main building and announced to all the boys at supper that there'd be no homework that night. They'd see *Gold Rush* instead and each boy could go to the canteen and pick out chips *and* a soda *and* a bar. All evening he felt naughty and proud. But he tossed and turned in bed, worried he'd acted out of false pride.

After the third man takes the stand, Gerard decides he can't keep thinking about the past. What good does it do, dredging up these old details? He's got things happening in his life right now that need attention, and all because of this trial. His lawyer has told him to keep taking notes. But everything that is being said has been already been said twice before and presumably will go around nine more times. The jurors are starting to look bored. They get sent out of the courtroom a lot while the lawyers argue whether certain lines of questioning should be allowed. Gerard has heard the sheriff's officers say the women are knitting up a storm during the time they wait downstairs in the jury room and that one of them brought in this cappuccino machine they're all going mad for.

The lawyers have settled into a steadiness, a matter-of-fact-ness. It has been five weeks now. They joke about being here for another three months.

Here I am just a bit taller than the door latch – I can feel it digging in back of my head – and here he is picking me up by my ears and telling me to clamp it or everything is going to hurt more.

More and more, all Gerard can think of is the pup and how it's doing. He remembers the little squeaky sound it makes when it yawns. He doesn't know why he got it with the trial coming up, but he did. He wasn't going to, but then the trial was postponed for the second time, some conflict with the judge's schedule. He just saw the pup – in a pet store, of all places – and took it home.

He'd felt like a new mother. Every sound led back to the pup. He was in the library one day when he was sure he could hear Brigus keening. Gerard had stood there waiting for claws to scrape white lines on his shins. But of course the dog wasn't there. The sound must have been a pencil sharpener or some such thing.

Walking home the long way, the pretty way – along the Avon and its low-waisted willows, past Tom Patterson Island, past the Stratford Festival Theatre, past the squirrels – another squeal from Brigus, except really it came from a gull. And the next false alarm was a scream of brakes from a bus.

When he'd returned home to the pup, a copy of *The Power and the Glory* warming his armpit, there was only the sound of his keys hitting the table and a metronome of tail hitting the sides of the crate. Thump thump thump thump, etc.

I never told no one until my lady put it on the line. She said, 'Look, my honey, you've got something eating you all these years and it's eating me too and I'm falling apart and I don't even know why.'

He wonders how the house-sitter is making out. He calls her a couple of times a week and she says everything's fine, but he wonders if that's really the case. It bothers him, having someone in his house. But what can he do? The pup can't be abandoned.

He'd put an ad in the paper for a caretaker. The girl answered and so did some older women and a boy maybe twenty-one. He interviewed the boy and liked him best, but decided against him on the basis of the trouble factor with boys. The women talked too much. The girl was quiet. He had her move in the week before he left just to make sure he could trust her. She didn't spend any time on the phone, which surprised him. She washed her dishes as soon as she finished eating. She spent all her time with the pup, mostly outside.

He'd told her he didn't know how long he'd be gone on business. Depended how the deal went. Not too long, he didn't think.

'You still working?' It was the only question she ever asked him. He'd nodded. At night, he could hear her drag the nightstand up against her door. She kept the pup in with her.

I said, 'Lord Jesus, take me out of this.' And then I tried with the razor. I really wanted it. I would picture Bro. Lundrigan walking past my casket getting all shaky.

Okay, he's not a saint. There are times he's picked Brigus up by the gruff and shook him and whacked him, once even in front of the girl. You can only trip down the stairs so many times with forty-eight ounces of stupidity skinning your heel. You can only pick up gummed toilet paper so many times off the living room floor, say good-bye to so many boots and tea towels. Gerard had taken to reading a book on dog training by some monks who raise and sell drug-sniffing German shepherds at their monastery in New York State. He'd read it at four-thirty in the morning, wide awake after taking the dog outside for its first shit of the day. While Gerard read, Brigus would curl tight, a potato bug on the floor next to the bedframe. The monks say to never give in to exasperation. Stay in control. *To stop biting, give the snout a firm but harmless shake. Expect a yelp of surprise. Hold the palm flat and ask for a lick instead. Praise your pup.*

Sometimes Gerard has grabbed the pup's snout just to make it cry out.

Brigus never seems to bite the girl. She's to dust and vacuum and scrub every week. No visitors. She'll be needing to keep the lawn cut and the garden tidy. 'You understand everything I'm paying you to do?' he'd said. She'd nodded. It was his parents' house, he told her, and needed to be treated with that kind of respect. She'd nodded again. The pup was to be her first priority, though. Another nod, this time with a slight smile attached.

He wonders if she's having parties. If there are people fornicating in his house right now. In his parents' old bed. He decides to call again at the lunch break.

No answer, for the fourth day in a row.

* * *

The fifth complainant knocks the hell out of him. Gerard has no idea who he is. He knows he didn't recognize the name, but he thought when he saw the fellow it would all click. The man hadn't made it to the prelim, and now that Gerard is finally looking right at him, he can't place him at all.

At lunch he says to his lawyer, 'How could I not know one of the children?'

His lawyer looks tired. 'What's to remember when you're dealing with a liar?'

The records point to Gerard teaching the man for three years – he apparently failed grade seven math. He's convinced the man must have had another name back then. How could Gerard forget one of the boys?

The lack of giving in the dog really surprised him. He wishes he could talk to the New York State monks about that. They'd know what he means. It sits there insisting on being noticed, forever complaining. Something the orphans never would have dared. Fat Brigus, ears flopping back and forth as he pisses on the bathmat, wants chicken, wrestling matches, lap naps, and cheese.

Surely the dog will still know him when he gets back?

He remembers the eleventh complainant in great detail. A sweet boy he was, needy but still sweet. Had these fat ringlets and a long skinny frame. Gerard's favourite possum, always leaning in, content. *Look what I got you, Brother.* And in his fist a wet stone, one side glowing an ashy red if the light hit it right. Gerard would pick him up and hold him tight.

He's grey now and has his hair clipped. Still thin, though. He would have loved Brigus, that boy, would have petted him bald. *If you pinches the pads on their feet they won't jump up no more, isn't that right? You gots to give them a big squirt of a*

*squeeze whenever they does that. Can I touch his tail, Brother?
I mean, may I, Bro.?*

The mother of the eleventh man gets herself in the paper.
Apparently she's been in the public gallery through the whole
trial. She waits until her boy's finished testifying. He has been
crying softly for the last hour or so on the stand. But the mother
doesn't go to her son. No, as soon as the judge leaves the courtroom, she walks up behind Gerard and tugs on the elbow of his
cardigan and explains who she is.

No one else has spoken to him, aside from his lawyer. The
reporters look down when he walks past them. The sheriff's
officers never speak directly to him. 'Does Mr Lundrigan want
some water?' they'll ask his lawyer. The clerks don't look at
him. Even in corner stores, if he's buying a paper or some
chocolate, no one looks right at him. Sometimes the cashier
won't hold her hand out to take the money, forcing him to leave
it on the counter and forget about the change.

But the mother smiles. 'I've forgiven you,' she says.

Gerard's lawyer moves closer.

'I've thought about it and you're going to do your time and
you should get at least one more little chance, you know. I
mean, who in frig am I to rebuke you? I mean, I'm the one who
handed over my boy, right?'

The spectators who are getting ready to put on their coats
are like hares, all ears and eyes.

The woman's voice is getting louder, too. 'I kept saying he's
just a man, same as any other. Just a man. That's how I'm going
to look at you, anyway. Others might not, but I'm going to. For
me, you know. For myself. Important, you know?'

Gerard turns from her, reaches for his coat.

She comes around on the other side so that she's still facing
him. The reporters are there now, too, holding out microphones.

'I mean nothing can give back my Sean what you took, so why should we keep after you, really? I mean, jail, yes. Go to jail for a while, you definitely should do that. But hatred, that's no good.'

'Okay, okay,' the sheriff's officers say. 'This courtroom's closed for the day.' They have their hands on her elbows and are edging her back, gently.

She says, 'Do you have a message I could bring to the boys for you?'

He puts his arms across his chest and hates himself for doing it.

'Len Stamps, Red Matthews, Tom Walsh. You remember them all, right? Plus my Sean, of course.'

The officers are getting her closer to the door. She's pushing against them.

'Donnie Hawko. Bill Wheaton, John Cooke, Vince Rutherford. You heard them. You heard what they said.'

The reporters are following her, trying to ask her questions. But she ignores them.

'Say you're sorry,' she yells. 'Say "I apologize." Just say that. You'll feel better.'

The next afternoon, Gerard is on the stand. The only witness for the defense. Some of the other Brothers wouldn't take the stand at their trials. But the juries didn't like that, apparently. Besides, Gerard doesn't mind talking. There's no way he can keep sitting on his hands.

The jury will see the authority he carries, the calm. The jury will remember the complainants and their mental illnesses, their criminal records. The roughness about them.

Except when he first gets on the stand, he feels like he might pass out. Everywhere he looks, he sees set faces.

He imagines the girl bringing Brigus here, coming in through the spectators' door and letting him off the lead at the back of the courtroom, a much bigger Brigus running at full hurl to cover Gerard with licks. He sees everyone smiling: the judge, the jury, the audience, himself. After that, he gets his confidence back. *We wanted those boys to have a chance in the world. We pushed them. We made it clear everything was going to be hard for them. We didn't believe in pretending they weren't orphans.*

On the Sunday before cross-examination is to start, the girl answers the phone. She tells him she's seen his picture in the paper. She says she'll take care of the dog no matter what but she doesn't know if she can stay in the house because it is too sickening. She is thinking about going home to her parents and taking Brigus with her. 'No,' Gerard says. 'You have to stay.' If she leaves, she could steal everything on her way out. She could write things on the walls. She could set the house on fire. She could take Brigus and never give him back.

'Who exactly are you to be setting the rules?' she says, and he understands then her quietness is not as peaceful as he'd thought.

All he can say is, 'Please, it's not whatever you're thinking.' And offer extra money.

The crown attorney mocks him. 'You mean, you taught this man for three years but can't remember him? Therefore, if you can't remember him, we're to conclude you're innocent? Okay, let's look at that. Let's say you couldn't remember whether you'd filed your income taxes for last year. Let's say it turns out you didn't. Does that mean, in the eyes of Revenue Canada, that you're off the hook, Mr Lundrigan?'

Gerard can only repeat what he's already said several times: 'I know the records indicate that man was in my classroom three years running, but I also know I'd never laid eyes on him before this trial started, so how could I have done these terrible things as he claims?'

The jury finds that amusing. The judge calls a break.

There's another bad moment on what turns out to be Gerard's last day of cross-examination. It involves the allegations of the last complainant, Sean.

'Did you ever, Mr Lundrigan, slip your tongue into his mouth as alleged?'

'No. But perhaps once when I kissed him there might have been an accident.'

'You kissed the boy?'

'Yes, many times. Like a mother.'

'On the lips?'

'Yes, sir. Like a mother would.'

'Did you kiss the other boys?

'No, sir.'

'Why not?'

'He was special, very dear to me, innocent. He needed affection.'

'So you kissed him on the lips?'

'I've already answered that.'

'Like a mother?'

'Like a mother.'

'Did you ever insert your penis into his mouth?'

'Of course not.'

'Even by accident?'

Gerard's lawyer objects, and the judge agrees. She calls an early lunch break.

Gerard's lawyer says he can't eat with him today – he has to run to the dentist. A weak lie since normally they'd still be in session.

Gerard sees Sean's mother putting on her coat in the last row of benches in the public gallery. He wouldn't let himself look over that way when he was on the stand. Now she won't look at him.

The judge gives her charge to the jury. It takes two days for her to finish. Gerard spends the time working on an apology to the boys, but nothing comes out right.

I have no malice towards you. You came to us robbed. We were only boys ourselves, you forget that.

I'm sorry you made me come here.

I'm sorry you've made such a fuss.

I'm sorry you want my blood.

To think he wiped their asses.

A pity his lawyer would never let him send a letter. It might help them.

The jury is out. Gerard's lawyer gives him a cell phone and tells him to stay within a ten-minute radius of the courtroom. The lawyer says not to fret if the deliberations take several days – the longer, the better. 'I'd hang out with you,' the lawyer says, 'but I'm just snow-balled with work at the office.'

At first Gerard stays in the little apartment he's rented. He knew the wait was going to be bad, but not this bad. If he lies on the bed, the ceiling comes down to a point just above his nose. The more he paces, the more he sees himself in the mirrors that are all over the room. If he looks out the window, he feels lonely.

The harbour is quiet. The *Astron* is in, and a fisheries patrol vessel. Some longliners. It is sunny, and even better, it's windy. Somehow the gusts comfort him. It's a clean wind here, a wind that leaves the good in you.

It licks at him as he starts winding up the road to Signal Hill. Maybe no one will recognize him with his ear flaps down. Not that he's hiding – it's the kind of cold that makes your ear drums ache.

The flags at Cabot Tower flap like tents in a blizzard. The few people walking around up here actually nod at him. It's a community of sorts, brought on by the elements.

He walks some more, looks down at Chain Rock. He could aim for it. There's no way he could even come close. But he could tell himself that's what he was doing. The wind would rub him against a rock face on the way down. If he waits until he's a bit colder he probably wouldn't feel a thing.

He remembers his last day with the dog. Not even that went right. He'd only meant to nudge Brigus toward the door with his foot but for some reason he'd kicked the pup good and hard. He'd spent forever trying to get it out from under the couch. In the end Gerard set up a semi-circle of cheese cubes, like stepping stones to the centre of the living room.

Outside, they'd passed through the art gallery grounds to get down to the river. Brigus barrelled through the steel sculpture that looks like an oversized napkin holder and then spun around, checking to make sure he could still see Gerard. When they got over the railroad tracks and down the hill, the dog hacked after studiously and sombrely licking a mound of dirt. Gerard had felt like whipping himself. 'I'm no good for you,' he'd said, and walked away, fast. But no matter where he stepped, he could hear the pup rushing the grass right behind.

What you do and what you mean. Two entirely different things. Gerard never meant anyone any trouble.

He does mean to push off right now, but he can't do it.

He heads down the footpath to the Interpretation Centre, where there are payphones – he's not allowed to tie up the cell phone. Gerard calls his house and, miraculously, she picks up.

'You're still there?' he says.

'I need the money, okay?'

'That's fine,' he says, 'I'm happy.'

No response.

Gerard tries again. 'He's your dog, okay? You take him. If you go.'

The wind makes him cry on the way back down the hill. It keeps grinding bits of dirt right in there. He's hurrying because he's just now understanding it's not going to take the jury long.

There's so much wind he wonders whether he'll even hear the phone if it rings in his pocket.

But he does. He's surprised how relieved he feels.

✎ Acknowledgements ✐

Many, many thanks to editor John Metcalf.

And to Saeko Usukawa.

Thanks also to: Luanne Armstrong, Janet Berketa, Libby Creelman, Frank Davey, Owen Dearing, Stephanie Dearing, Susan Dearing, Ross Deegan, Olga Dzatko, Jack Eastwood, Dilshad Engineer, Mark Ferguson, Michael Gardner, Zsuzsi Gartner, Jessica Grant, Jane Hamilton, Quade Hermann, Diane Humber, Larry Jackson, Wayne Johnston, Mike Jones, Ed Kavanagh, Thomas King, Chris LaBonté, Andrea MacPherson, Keith Mallaird, Larry Mathews, Ellen McGinn, George McWhirter, Lisa Moore, Jean Rysstad, Beth Ryan, Craig Takeuchi, Madeleine Thien, Peggy Thompson, Pauline Thornhill, Claire Wilkshire, Michael Winter, Patricia Young. Thanks to the B.C. Arts Council for support.

Earlier versions of some of the stories in this collection have appeared in the following places: 'Giulione's Zipper' in *The Fiddlehead*, and 'Fascia' in *The Malahat Review*. 'So Beautiful the Firemen Would Cry' was printed first in *Prairie Fire*, and then in *Best Canadian Stories: 02*. 'St. Jerome' won at the Newfoundland and Labrador Arts and Letters Competition in 2002. Oberon's *Coming Attractions: 01* picked up 'Getting a Message Through to the Girl' and 'The Simple Truth'. Oberon also printed 'An Apology' in *Best Canadian Stories: 01*, 'Itty Bitty Road' in *Best Canadian Stories: 98* and 'Little Spanks' in *Best Canadian Stories: 97* (this story was later reprinted in the Killick anthology, *Hearts Larry Broke*).

JANET BERKETA

Ramona Dearing lives in St. John's, Newfoundland. Her poems and short stories have appeared in the *Malahat Review, Grain* and *Prairie Fire*, as well as in Oberon's *Best Canadian Stories* (1997, 1998 and 2001) and *Coming Attractions* (2001). She is a member of the fiction collective the 'Burning Rock' and is represented along with Lisa Moore, Michael Winter, and Claire Wilkshire in the Burning Rock anthology *Hearts Larry Broke*. She works for CBC Radio.